WHEN PLANETS SLIP THEIR TRACKS

To Jackie,

I hope you enjoy 'When Planets Slip Their Tracks'!

with warmest wishes,

Joanna Campbell

x.

Other books by this author

TYING DOWN THE LION

WHEN PLANETS SLIP
THEIR TRACKS

Joanna Campbell

Ink Tears
The Granary,
Purston,
Brackley,
Northants,
NN13 5PL

ISBN 978 1910207 062

British Library Cataloguing in Publication Data.
A catalogue record for this book is available from the British Library.

Typeset by Troubador Publishing Ltd
Printed and bound by CPI Group (UK) Ltd, Croydon, CR0 4YY

For Adrian, Alexandra, Olivia and Georgia; Mum, Dad and Chris.

CONTENTS

When Planets Slip Their Tracks   1
Solid Orange Sea   6
Cherry's Stain   18
Before Last Wednesday   28
Decisions Made Over Madeleine's Toast   37
Wind and Water   45
Big Day Out   54
A Safe House For Elephant Ten   65
The Reliable Sitter   69
The Invitation   77
One-Horse Town   84
Quiston Avenue   90
The Biology Lesson   99
Aurora and the Book Trolley   106
The Revival of Clara Petacci   114
Michael's List Of Fears   122
The English Lesson   130
The Long Drive   139
Bonanza Tully's Baby   147
Following Candace   156
Opening Time   164
Ten O'clock to Balham   173
Before The Birds Sing   181
Half-Price Mondays With Hélène   185
Acknowledgements   193

WHEN PLANETS SLIP THEIR TRACKS

Nate knew how to hypnotise a chicken. But he knew next to nothing about me. Didn't matter none when we were growing up in Stone Gap. Still had the same old dirt in our dungarees nigh on every day. Long, dusty summers never ended. But only I knew how I loved the bones of that boy.

Our classmates whooped when Nate laid the chick in the dirt, holding its thin feet firm in one hand. Mouths wide, they watched his finger trace a line in the earth, straight from the beak. The bird's beady eye followed the course of Nate's line like he was leading it to Heaven. Twenty full seconds it was down there in a trance.

All I recall is how tender Nate held it, his fingers curved around the frail wings before he let it free.

Me and Nate had a baby, but we didn't know a thing about that. Just saw I was looking bonny and kind of ripe in the months after the rains.

"Have to shelter us in the cow-shed, is all," Nate had said. And I swear he had no notion in his head but keeping our hides dry. Our clothes steamed in the straw, while our bodies took charge of one another.

He didn't know he was in my head all the time. When we were playing out together or running errands to Hardwick's Mercantile, he didn't know I was thanking God in heaven for my friend Nate.

When he found the tender side of his self by the lake one fine June day, making may-apple flower chains to lace round my neck, I paid no heed to the twisting ways of my heart. It would always feel that way. And I just prayed Nate would feel it when we were grown.

Nate could swim in winter waters. He stripped and dove in, long white body scoring through the blank lake. Used to cut right in there with him when I was a little child.

But when we were fifteen and the baby inside began to show, my shame grew right along there with it. My swaying belly weren't fit to be seen naked.

"Get in that water, girl," Nate said. "I like it."

He held out his hand and I went in. The cold lake lapped over the little mound. Nate wrapped his fingers round it. He was the first of us to feel the baby squirm.

Never swam after the birthing. I missed the quickening of new life in my soul. And the love burning through the shame. I was lost after the baby was buried. Fit for nothing. If I'd stepped into that water, I'd have kept right on walking, deeper and deeper to the middle, until my head was under and my memories soaked through.

Nate knew the stars. He had a connection with them, like he was in a book, a magic-boy with a string binding him to the Milky Way.

Some nights we lay on the wet grass by the lake and drifted up there. The sky came right down low above our eyes. The more we stared with no blinking, the more stars we could see. Like they were fire-spiders pulling us up inside their web, weaving us into their blue nets full of light. I was less off-course on those nights with Nate. I felt found again.

On our last day of school, we roamed our best places until dark, feet bare and holding hands. Nate rolled up his certificate like a telescope.

"I can see for freakin' miles," he said. His voice was rasping with hopes. And I could feel a tremble in his thigh against mine. Starred nights were Nate's favourite time.

"I can think straight. See a path."

That's what he always said. His destiny wouldn't be the coal-face always. He knew it and so did I.

Never wanted nothing more than to walk that path with Nate. Never did say it though. Had no right to push myself on someone with a brain and a dream and a path.

And that's why Nate knew nothing about me. He could read the stars. He could bewitch a chicken. But shutters were latched on my thoughts. No folk allowed there. Not even Nate.

All the lake days and waist-high cornfield days and blue-star nights went away when school finished.

"Get that broom sweeping, Carrie. Don't pay you for thinking, do I?"

That's what Aunt Lawrence always says. She thinks I'm lucky to have work. Lucky my folk didn't kill me when they saw my little baby, blue in the bedclothes. She puts the mop in my hand before I'm up her steps. Before I'm level with the stone lion by her door. Thrusts it at me like I'm wild boar rampaging on her dandy lawn.

That's my life. A circle, it is. Day begins in the old chicken-house in back of Aunt Lawrence's. Round to her door, my head hanging low in gratitude. Up the two mile track to my old school to boil dinners. Down the other side of the valley to Hardwick's to bruise my knees wiping the butchery floor at the tail-end of a day's slaughter.

Hardwick likes me using rags, watching from behind while I'm down there, backside in the air. Sassy Clements works on confectionery by the window. Other end from me. You need clean pig-tails and white petticoats for that. Hardwick gave her a straw hat with silk ribbons. 'Hershey Milk Chocolate Kisses' is what's printed in pink on the brim.

She gives me a hard smile when she finishes for the day. Bites off the head of a sugar mouse. Pitches the hat on a hook behind her counter. I watch it swing after she skips out the door, the shop bell jangling long after she's gone.

Now we're grown, it's hard to get a glimpse of Nate. When I stand up to rinse the bloodied cloths, I see him pass by. A flash of his moon-lit yellow hair on winter nights as he strides home from the coal-face. A dark blur of wide woollen shoulders when the fog comes down.

In summer I see more. The air is sweeter. The hedge-rows are frosted with the black powdered sugar of coal dust. Nate looks in and waves. Sassy spins round and waves back. Looks at me with triumph blaring from her pebbly eyes. But, sure as slow-worms, his wave is meant for me.

One day he goes by clean. His face is peach-skin, like when we were kids. Sassy rustles her Baby Ruth candy bars and nestles them in a box. She turns to blow him a kiss. And he smiles at her. Then at me. And it's a sorry smile.

I never had a sorry from no one before. And it means he knows. He must have cranked open those shutters of mine without me realising. One of those times by the lake where the dank skunk-cabbage and squirrel-corn brawl over the earth, leaves lolloping all over. One of those times when we looked into each other and Stone Gap all but disappeared. Alls I knew was how deep I loved him. He must have known it too. I can tell by his sad smile and the way his eyes glance in shame at Sassy's white apron.

Sitting in my coop that night, I heard the overgrown grass whisper. Still knew his tread. He came in there and smoothed the hair from where it fixed wet to my cheeks. He kissed both my eyelids. His lips left a print. Then he took my hand and we went out together for the last time.

"We can have us a marriage ceremony right here. Once that the

4

good Lord won't see, sorry to tell. Private for just you and me," he said.

So down we went to the edge of the lake and let the sky be our witness and the screech-owl our preacher. Just how the first wedding in the world must have been. Nate said, "I'll love you even when the planets slip their tracks."

And he fashioned a bit of old metal into a circle that fitted my finger fine as any ring from the fancy goods store. And we looked way out over the glass surface of the water that begged to be broken by our bare bodies.

"That sure as God is perfect," Nate said, watching me.

I began to pull off my dress. He stopped me, his hand gentle on mine.

"Best keep it that way," he said, looking to the horizon that marked the endless beginning of his journey. A firm faraway line separating the smooth water and the endless reach of the sky.

And that was where our marriage had to end.

His wedding to Sassy took place next day in a hard cloud of white rice. Day after that, he became Teller in her Pa's bank. The baby was coming by Christmas. He had his path laid out neat, did Nate.

And I stayed under his spell. Always will. Said 'I do' and meant it. Just the same as Sassy meant it when she spoke the same words in her lace gown and orange-blossoms.

Cleaning, boiling, toiling, kneeling. Round in a circle like a chicken in the yard and back to the coop every day. Sundays tending our baby's little spot under the sycamores of Stone Gap church-yard. Thinking how my Nate out there in the city knew me all the time. And wearing my wedding ring 'til the planets slip their tracks.

Solid Orange Sea

After two lessons, Madame Beryl requested that Clemency leave, never to return. She had picked up a large white tap-shoe that belonged to an older girl with woman-sized feet. Theo saw her finger trace the outline of the metal sole-plate, bumping over the nail-heads that held it in place.

Mother had been distracted, reading a notice about a forthcoming show with parts for all girls and requests for mothers to make tutus.

"Clemency, put it down," Theo said. "Madame Beryl's watching you."

Clemency smiled at Theo and flung the tap-shoe at Madame Beryl's head.

Theo thought it most fortunate that Madame Beryl wore ear-muffs for protection from the thunder of tap class. They prevented the bruising from being more severe than it was.

Clemency would never blossom. Not with that face. It wasn't a damaged face. It was just very messy. But Theo was used to it. Unlike Mother, who seemed to think she would wake Clemency one momentous morning to find Grace Kelly gazing up at her.

Theo showed Clemency to his friends when they came for tea because they paid him. And if they played Monopoly, he declared himself banker and cheated her out of thousands of pounds.

"Shame on you, Theo," Mother said once when she spotted the pink edge of a £500 note in his sock.

Theo didn't think Clemency should be a Brownie. It would lead to disappointment. She waved her wild arms when Mother showed her the bottom-hole-brown uniform. She grabbed the yellow scarf thing and the flat pancake hat and flung them at the wall, where they hung, almost pleasingly, on the beaks and wings of the three brass flying ducks. She screamed at the shoes with laces she would never master. Theo wondered if she knew she would never blend into a pack.

When Clemency was enrolled, he had to go with Mother to watch. She recited the Promise in her gruff, old-man voice. Georgina, a big girl with two yellow plaits, held Clemency's hand for the skipping round the toadstool part. Theo swallowed a hateful gristle thing in his throat when he saw her lumbering round it, hanging onto Georgina's polite hand.

At the end, when Brown Owl dismissed the pack at the church-hall doors, she slid a box of orange-flavour Matchmakers into Georgina's pocket.

It was always raining on Brownie nights. Mother struggled to hold the umbrella and restrain Clemency from running at cars or stopping to see everything her great big feet trod on. Daisies, drains, cigarette packets, conkers, gobbets of chewing-gum in the gutter. Her eyes were always on the ground and her head in the clouds. Theo didn't think it possible to do both at once.

Theo begged to stay at home and be shot of her. But once he was alone, his sigh of contentment made a lonely echo. He longed to spread out his post office without Clemency insisting she must be his only customer. He wanted people of his own invention to come in and out. With Clemency around he couldn't separate stamps along their perforations or rubber-stamp dog-licences or weigh matchbox-parcels on the plastic scales. She always took his ink-pads and his thumb-pad for note counting and hid them under the floorboards in her room. Last Monday, he'd also unearthed his peanut-brittle and the wing she'd snapped off his Messerschmitt.

Yet with the house to himself, the post office waited in vain for him to open it. The bell for customers to tap when they arrived at the kitchen-table didn't ring.

When Mother came home from delivering Clemency to Brownies, Theo stood close to her in the kitchen, watching her roll pastry or skin oranges for caramelising. He felt the strips of oily peel in his fingers before she infused them in hot sugar water. The pan released a sweet tang that soaked the kitchen until they were wading in orange sea. Theo closed the door to keep in his and Mother's ocean.

When the oranges in their syrup were chilling in the fridge, she glanced at the clock, gathered her gloves and opened the door to the hall. Cold air rushed in.

"Mother, will you come to my post office please?"

"Oh, Theo, be sensible. Look at the time."

"There's ages yet."

"She likes me to hear her sing 'Day Is Done'."

"She doesn't actually *sing* it, does she?"

"Of course she does. She loves singing," Mother said, her headscarf fluttering in her fingers as if desperate to escape.

Theo wondered if the other Brownies raised their eyebrows at Clemency's bullfrog baritone.

After Mother left, Theo shut himself in the kitchen again, breathing the orange-fragranced air.

One dark, wet night when she came home, Mother said, "Oh Theo, Clemency wants to take the Golden Hand test like all the other girls. There are sixteen tasks to perform. She would earn a badge I could sew onto her sleeve."

"Does she have to?"

"Oh, Theo, it's not that she *has* to. In fact, Brown Owl did rather try to dissuade her. I felt so cross. You see, she wants to do this. And you'll want to encourage her, won't you, Theo? Please help."

Theo watched his mother plead with him, a compass clutched in her hand. Clemency had to learn to set eight of its points. In her other hand she held two flags borrowed from Brown Owl. Clemency had to interpret the entire alphabet in semaphore, as well as send and read three out of four letters. Mother furnished Theo with the Brownie handbook so that he could teach her.

It disrupted Saturdays. No more Monopoly, Mother said. But Clemency wouldn't let Theo hold the compass to explain its points. She clutched it to her chest and shrieked. She wanted to do it all herself and for Theo to watch her. She refused to let him touch the flags or see the diagrams in the book.

"How can I help if you won't let me?" he roared in frustration one day when Mother was picking loganberries in the back garden. "You're just a joke. You'll never pass the test."

Mother came in. "Clemency needs time," she said. "She'll get there in the end, Theo. Remember the way I explained it to you? If she were swimming, she would need to tread water for a while even if all the others have already struck out to sea."

"But she'll never even doggy-paddle," Theo said. "She knows she's different."

"Nonsense," Mother said as if Clemency was about to launch into a perfect butterfly stroke and leave the others gasping like stranded fish on the sand.

Theo was removed from his duties. All Golden Hand preparations shifted to the front-room. Mother shut herself and Clemency in there all weekend and every evening, emerging only on Wednesdays for Brownies, when she put Theo in charge of watching a frozen meat pie bake in the oven.

He went into the front-room in between pie-watching. It looked so different. Normally Mother only let them use it at

Christmas. Theo had only ever seen it with a paper-chain attached to the pelmet.

The tasks were listed in red felt-tip pen on a sheet of paper taped to the wall.

Singing
Plant growing
Wrapping
Knitting
Bandaging
Folding
Tea making
Communication

The first and last verses of 'God Save the Queen' were written in red crayon on sugar-paper and stuck to the sideboard. On a high shelf, a fat hyacinth in a white pot stood to attention. Theo could just see the first defenceless fingertip of purple piercing its tight, leafy glove.

A box covered in brown paper was loosely tied with frayed string and smothered with attempts at writing an address.

A woollen scarf was growing. Mother's needles sent echoes up to Theo's room at midnight, their clicking syncopated with the ticking of his alarm-clock as she tightened the scarf's slack stitches.

Two semaphore flags lay exhausted on the coffee-table. A crumpled diagram showed the different positions.

The flags never overlap, except when in the rest position.

Theo placed one over the other, crossing the sticks and smoothing the little cotton pennants flat.

Semaphore conveys information at a distance.

He imagined Clemency's arms, like a windmill in a tornado, conveying nothing at all.

At weekends, Theo was shut out of the kitchen while they

cooked milk-puddings. The sweet smell seeped under the door, reminding him of the beaker of warm milk a teacher gave him the day he fell off the climbing-frame. The minute-hand of the sick-room clock made shuddering progress, reminding him of his sister in her orthopaedic shoes. The sound of time began to feel awkward and testy. The sick-room became his own head.

He'd stayed at home the next day, feeling sick and dizzy. Mother made him lie in bed and read a book. But it hurt his eyes and none of the words made sense. Clemency was having one of her attacks with her tongue lolling and her eyes on stoppers, so he didn't tell Mother how he felt. She had too much to do.

Since that day, he had always felt he was sliding down a ladder. He was taken to a special class once a week and assigned to a helper who looked at him as if he were a slice of fruit-cake on a plate. Rather a stale fruit-cake. She leafed through his science and maths books, explaining things they both thought he should already know.

The front-room became home to the ironing-board and the teapot, the shoe-polishing kit and the first-aid box. Piles of clothes for folding practice filled the settee. The contents of all other rooms moved there. With Mother's guidance, Clemency drew the Golden Hand symbol and Mother painted it with gold paint borrowed without asking from Theo's model aeroplane kit.

It was a strange hand, Theo thought. The little finger and its neighbour were bent in towards the palm, as was the thumb. The other two fingers stood up straight in what appeared to Theo to be a menacing gesture, a hostile salute. Mother taped it to the front-room door. Although the piles of plants, clothes, bandages and parcels meant the door could barely open anyway, the Hand stopped Theo in his tracks.

The front lawn became a practice arena for ball-throwing and skipping. With chalk from Theo's art box Mother marked a line for Clemency to attempt tossing a ball overarm for a distance of seven yards. She also had to skip backwards, turning the rope thirty times, and learn complex feet-crossing and toe-pointing skills. The lawn turned into a battlefield.

Theo noticed how the neighbours shut their windows. And ladies on their way to the shopping-parade crossed to the other side of the road, even though it meant passing the bench where the staring man in broken trousers asked, "Want to see my noodle, Missus?"

Ten balls met their death under tyres. Eight more lodged in the gutter. And one stuck inside the chimney, dislodging a brittle pigeon. And one wet Saturday when Mother suggested going back inside, Clemency seized the skipping-rope and tried to throttle her.

Mother began leaving Theo a salad for tea on the kitchen table. She popped out of the front-room to say hello when he came in from school, but the Golden Hand drew her back within seconds.

Sometimes Theo picked up the barrette that used to grip her hair into a chignon. It lay on the shelf in the hall with her lipstick. When Theo held them in his hand, the memory of their shapes remained in the dust. He replaced them in their exact spot, so she'd know where to find them.

One afternoon, he arrived home to find Mother in tears. He wanted to turn round and go back to school. Mothers didn't cry. And it wasn't that discreet motherly eye-dabbing with a handkerchief during a film about love. This was a clotted track of snot, and eyes that were small and selfish-red.

Three things had occurred.

The front room was badly scorched after Clemency's bid to grasp the fire-lighting skills. Mother had been heating milk in the kitchen for Clemency's ninth attempt at junket, pleading with her to wait, to sit on her hands. Mother thought she had hidden the matchbox, but Clemency could sniff out a match from fifty paces.

The curtains were black. Much of their practice equipment was smoke-damaged. There were holes in Brown Owl's flags.

As if that weren't enough, one of the firemen told Mother that his Debbie had worked like a Trojan to earn the badge last summer because it was being phased out this year. No more retakes if anyone failed. It was all a matter of time. Take your chance or lose it.

It was a tough test, he said. He hoped Clemency's inferno wouldn't hold her back. He hoped the Golden Hand would shine on her sleeve like it did on his Debbie's.

"So little time," Mother said, her voice thickening again. "If Clemency fails, she'll be devastated."

Theo imagined the fireman's Debbie with the Golden Hand sticking its two fingers up on her sleeve.

Mother wept into her apron. Theo had to wait a minute to hear the third problem.

Mother had telephoned Brown Owl to pour her heart out. She'd sounded slurred, as if Mother had woken her from a nap. Everyone knew that an affection for the sherry bottle had caused Brown Owl to doze off during church parade and hiccup throughout the hovercraft trip from Ramsgate to Calais.

"I asked if Clemency should take time off school to study for her test," Mother said. "And do you know, Theo, Brown bloody Owl said it didn't matter – *didn't matter* – if Clemency failed. She said it was only one small day out of Clemency's life."

The 'one day' was the real issue for Mother. She had assumed the sixteen parts of the test would be spread over a few weeks. There was not the slightest chance of Clemency boiling milk and bandaging a femur on the same day. Let alone all the other demands as well. Just doing up the brown paper parcel tied her in knots. And made her likely to swear. Possibly even claw at the examiner's cardigan.

"That's the rule," Brown Owl had insisted before hanging up and almost certainly returning to her crystal glass which, whenever anyone called, was hastily hidden on her bookcase, behind a battered copy of *Jinty's Patrol*.

Life changed even more for Theo. While the plasterers wielded their trowels in the front-room, Clemency and Mother practised hell-for-leather upstairs. At least Mother did.

Theo set up his post office on the kitchen table. Sometimes the ceiling rattled so hard the weights fell off his scales. He issued the painter or the electrician with miniature letters to post in his pillar-box, which was an Ovaltine tub painted red.

Theo's life would change back, he was sure, once the Golden Hand withdrew.

But the day came when Mother discovered that although Clemency could present the fully-developed hyacinth - only lightly fire-damaged – that she was supposed to have tended herself, all Golden-Handers must whip up their puddings from scratch. The judges would scrutinise their ability to grate nutmeg and soak gelatine leaves. That way, Mothers couldn't whip up blancmanges and let daughters wobble them in front of the adjudicating panel as if they were all their own work. Nor could they take a ready-wrapped parcel or a pre-folded mackintosh. It wouldn't just be the semaphore and the ball-throwing the judges would test on The Day, but most of the other skills too. This was because the Golden Hand was all about managing life within a time-frame, with one's golden hands.

Mother had thought she was on the verge of holding the Golden Hand in hers. Cheating had been the only option. She had considered that if all was fair in love and war, then the same rule could apply to Brownie badge-earning. At least where Clemency was concerned, it could. Now she was a desperate woman. Theo heard the weeping that proved it.

Mother stopped sleeping. She paced through the house, protesting that this was Clemency's golden opportunity to learn what it was like to be the same as everyone else.

And the final crushing blow was a casual comment from Joy, the carpenter's daughter. She popped in with her father's flask while he was rehanging the front-room door. A Brownie for years, she was now a seasoned Girl Guide. She'd warmed her hands around more camp-fires than electric ones, sat on more toadstools than armchairs. She possessed every badge from House Orderly to Stargazer.

"Oh, my proudest badge is my Golden Hand," she said. "It gave me my Wings."

"Wings?" Mother said.

"Oh yes. With my Wings I flew up to Girl Guides. Without the Hand, a Brownie just walks there."

Afterwards, Mother was unable to erase the image from her mind. "I can't bear it," she said. "Clemency will be the only Brownie to plod onwards instead of soaring."

Clemency overheard. She tore her painting to shreds. She drenched the hyacinth with Mother's fortified wine. She wrenched off the bandages that Mother had tied tight round her knees and elbows as permanent reminders of how to wind them. She threw up her junket. She smashed all the balls hard into the cucumber frame. She tossed all the cucumbers into the road where they were flattened in the rush-hour.

Theo felt the clutch of the Golden Hand loosen. Its two tyrannical fingers were folding into its palm. Its reign was over.

Mother began sleeping late on Saturdays, just like last year when the ballet-classes ended. Released from the stricture of the Hand, Clemency beamed at her brother again and even looked pretty sometimes.

"Want to play Monopoly?" Theo asked one Saturday while Mother was resting upstairs. "You can take Bill's place now he's finished distempering the ceiling. His piece is the dog, your favourite. Look, he's already got a full set of stations and a Get out of Jail Free card."

After she had thrown all his houses across the kitchen and pressed his hotels into the cat's meat, Theo let her be his post office assistant. But only if she promised not to run off with his blotter.

It rained hard that afternoon and the power cut out. Clemency unearthed Theo's torch from her floorboards, along with his fold-up chess-set and Micky Mouse egg-cup. Now she wasn't a Brownie, she was happy to surrender the hoard. It had been so hard, skipping round the toadstool while Theo caramelised oranges with Mother.

The only sound was the rain on the flat kitchen roof as they posted letters into the Ovaltine tin and wrote telegrams. Clemency's writing was a senseless sprawl of ink. But Theo didn't mind the mess because of the peace. Anyway, his own writing often didn't always make sense these days.

Clemency went away for a few minutes to fetch the burnt and blistered semaphore flags and had a wild practice session in the corner of the kitchen. She came back to the table and, as the daylight faltered, sang her Brownie evening song to Theo.

She still didn't know the tune well and the words were horribly muddled, but she sang until her voice became gravel. Theo cut a sweet orange into segments and she sucked them between verses as if it were half-time in a contest.

The Brownie song had nothing to do with beckoning golden fingers. The way she sang it, it had nothing much to do with anything. But Theo noticed how Clemency closed her eyes when she sang the line about feeling safe. And it was the only bit she actually sang correctly.

Day is dung, dog has swum,
Frothy snakes, frothy heels, frothy sigh.
Poorly swell, safely rest.

She missed out the line about God being nigh that was meant to end the song. She said He had nothing to do with anything she knew.

Mother had always insisted she must join in with the entire

16

song, but Theo assured her that people had the right to leave out words that didn't feel right.

This guarantee brought a great sense of relief and seemed to encourage her. Substituting the name of the *Blue Peter* dog, she proceeded to sing 'Petra Save the Queen' followed by 'Oh Morph Our Help in Ages Past'.

Theo hadn't realised before that Clemency actually thought about things. He applauded her, while she accepted a pretend bouquet with a gesture that was almost graceful.

She picked up the tattered flags. She gave Theo the book with the diagrams and stood so close to him he could feel a breeze from the path of the flags through the air.

She signed him four words, holding each letter steady for a long time, so Theo would be in no doubt. He found he could concentrate better than he'd been able to for a long time.

When she laid the flags down, she made sure she overlapped them and came back to the table with her almost-pretty smile. Even though her clumsy great feet kicked his ankle, Theo decided he wouldn't let his friends pay to laugh at her anymore.

She was supposed to sign from further away than their tiny kitchen allowed. But the Golden Hand wasn't in charge now. And Clemency had still conveyed vital information at a distance.

T-H-A-N-K Y-O-U M-Y T-H-E-O

CHERRY'S STAIN

Magda checked the new name in her diary. Cherry Marshall. Cherry was a colleague of Alison Smedley, a satisfied customer who wanted to stop her hands trembling when she played the piano in public. Magda had worked her magic. She made Alison believe she was someone else when she sat on the piano stool, someone bold in a glittering cape. Now Alison wanted the same spell cast for Cherry.

For years, Magda had paced up and down before a client arrived, wearing a channel in the carpet, like a mistress waiting for the crunch of her lover's shoes on the gravel path. But with Kevin gone, the juicy anticipation had withered. Clients bled together like a spreading bruise. They whined rather than talked. And left her feeling tender and dented like bad fruit. Afterwards she still cooked and read and ironed, but without Kevin it was like sitting in the full sun without a cool drink or a square of shade. No contrast. No relief.

She lit the lamp, its glow diffusing in a pool across her table. Evening clients suited her well. The amber light induced confidence where none existed. They wore their struggle like a rough cloak that slid off once they sank into the throne-like chair with its velvet-effect cushioning. Her own seat, one of the dining-room set, was lower, lending the client an authority they did not usually own.

Magda pulled her tunic on over her grey jersey. The good heather wool added to the effect. Clients opened up more than they would to a suit or a severe blouse.

She straightened the row of photographs and 'thank-you' cards on the shelf behind her chair. The smiling images and gilt lettering glinted. She adjusted the blind to filter out the last of the sun. The room should wrap itself around her clients. They shouldn't wish to leave when the clock struck the end of their hour.

"Cherry Marshall," Magda said aloud. It sounded full and ripe and feminine. Not like a person for whom life had turned sour.

When the bell rang, the tone held promise. Tentative like all new clients, but with a note of relief and resolution, as if Cherry Marshall had waited all her life to stand on this doorstep and have her problem swept away.

Magda repositioned the blind, allowing thin lines of sun to make a bright ladder across the table. She opened the door to a portly woman in a soft printed frock, whose generous smile flickered with nerves. A large birthmark, a port-wine stain, smothered approximately half her face.

"Miss Magda Cutts? I'm Cherry Marshall for the six o'clock appointment. I hope I'm not late. The traffic's come to an absolute standstill on the main road."

Magda pictured the congested street full of cars, their windows wound down and pink elbows protruding. She imagined Cherry, patient in a taxi, consoling the tired driver.

Although she didn't usually offer tea to clients, Magda decided to fill the kettle.

"Please come through. Would you like a cup of tea?" She pinpointed Cherry's grey eyes with her own, obliterating the port-wine stain from her vision.

Cherry sat in Magda's seat.

"Wouldn't you be more comfortable here?" Magda asked, indicating the higher chair.

"Oh, I thought that one would be yours, Miss Cutts. I'm so sorry, have I plonked myself down in the wrong place? Typical!"

The port-wine was rippled with worry.

"Not at all. No, please sit where it's most comfortable, Miss Marshall."

"Oh, Cherry, please."

"Ah, very well. Cherry then. And I'm Magda."

She wasn't usually Magda for clients.

Even the room seemed different from the other chair. Magda could see the faded print of her and Kevin at the harbour café, laughing faces barely containing their fresh, bursting secret.

"It's this wretched public speaking, you see, Miss Cutts," Cherry was saying. "My job requires me to talk at conferences and I'm afraid I just crumple. Gibberish comes pouring out of my mouth." Cherry punctuated her words with great laughs and gestures, bracelets tinkling and perfume wafting. "I can't hold notes on a piece of paper because my hands shake. I don't understand it. I can talk until the cows come home, you know. Well, I expect you can tell that. But only in situations like this. In a room with just one other person, I'm fine. But once I stand up and look at a sea of faces with their eyes all fixed on me, I become a jelly."

Magda forgot to sit in her customary pose, which was leaning forwards in a manner that inspired trust, yet was not intimidating. She wasn't sure she'd remembered to give a brief nod now and then as proof she was listening. She simply drank Cherry in. Her fat, silver locket and pink summer dress, her honey-blonde fringe and aroma of freesia, they all quenched Magda's brittle solitude. This was an easy client. She didn't grouse. She seemed almost companionable.

Magda poured the tea and offered shortbread. She let crumbs scatter on her tunic. She didn't shoo away the cat when it sidled in and leapt onto Cherry's lap.

"Oh, I love cats, Miss Cutts. His fur's like silver velvet, isn't it?

Can he stay? I can't keep cats in my flat, but we're moving soon to a proper house. Since my promotion, we've been saving for a deposit. It's so exciting. But I won't keep my nice new salary unless I can hold my own at meetings. I'm looking forward to these sessions so much."

Cherry had faith in being cured. Magda could feel it in the room, as certain as the gradual decline of the lemony sunlight.

"So, I'm in your hands, Miss Cutts. I've tried relaxation tapes and yoga. But if you suggest those, of course I'll give them another go."

Compliant Cherry. The ideal evening client. Someone mouldable. Magda would finish the day with satisfaction for once.

Naturally, she would build self-esteem with practice talks. Record Cherry's voice to show how gifted she was at speaking. Urge her to attach notes to a stiff clipboard so the paper didn't flutter in her fingers. Work on a good stance, so she slid into her conference role like an actress.

"I am a public speaker," Cherry would need to repeat out loud to the mirror every day.

But maybe not to the mirror in her case. Magda wouldn't mention mirrors at all.

By the fifth or sixth session, she would suggest the thick make-up Cherry could purchase via mail-order. A peach shade rather than beige, to compliment the unblemished segment of her complexion. Blending it well would be vital. And a selection of soft scarves to drape around her neck and cast clever shadows across her face. A new hairstyle to fall over her cheeks and fan her neck. Camouflage was the key.

As a rule, Magda didn't discuss appearance with clients. She worked on their inner discomforts, following her training-manual to the letter.

"Why do I need to shout at an empty room, Miss Cutts?" one client had asked. "I'll feel daft. How will that help me believe in myself?"

"Surely a stiff brandy would get me through my oral exam better than this visualisation thingy?" another said. "Or should I visualise the brandy bottle, Miss Cutts?"

Cherry was unique, her barrier plain. Magda's usual methods were scarcely necessary. Cherry would savour the attention, the care. She was probably overlooked far too often. Magda watched her try the 'planting' exercise, which involved standing with her feet wider apart and her torso more upright for greater balance and breathing control.

Such a nice young woman when you know to look deeper, Magda pondered. *Such a shame people don't always look past disfigurements and see the person beneath.*

★

"That turquoise frock suits you," Magda said at the start of the third session. "The little frills are nicely distracting."

Cherry arched her eyebrows, still smiling.

"Distracting?" she said, her tone quizzical. "Isn't that a bad thing, Magda? If people concentrate on *me*, rather than my words, I shall lose my audience. They'll miss the salient points. You know, I once attended a lecture given by a terribly good-looking man in a tight shirt. And I'm ashamed to say I wanted to grab him and squeeze him tight! Hardly listened to a word he said, I must confess. Not his fault, but less revealing clothes might have helped."

She laughed in her grand style, clenching and unclenching her hands to demonstrate the tempting curve of his pectorals.

Magda felt moved by Cherry's performance. As if a man would notice her, other than to shudder! She had probably misunderstood the reference to distraction on purpose. Perhaps Magda had drawn attention to the stain too soon. She would leave well alone. She had got away with it, for now.

★

By session four, Cherry's warmth and lack of pretension had made her into a friend. She had twice overstayed her hour to accept Magda's invitation to coffee and pretzels. Magda had felt so empowered by the friendship, she felt able to mention Kevin and the loss of their baby.

Cherry took burdens without gasping. She listened as intently as a faithful dog, motionless and attentive. She said little and never offered pity. She simply let Magda feel the relief of shedding her load. Cherry couldn't spirit Kevin and the baby back. But she could absorb the grief like blotting-paper soaking up ink.

It was the fifth week when Magda showed Cherry the harbour picture. "We had just found out we were expecting a child. We were alive with the bliss of it. Other people seemed stripped of colour. We felt like golden celebrities. If anyone had brushed against us, our good luck would have touched them."

At the sixth meeting, Magda showed Cherry the white wool she had bought to knit a bonnet. "I haven't been able to get this out until now. But I wanted to show you. I feel ready. I was halfway through knitting this row when I felt the blood. I was frozen here on this sofa, watching my dream seep away." Magda fingered the soft wool between her fingers. "Kevin was supportive at first. So calm. I was mad with grief. But eventually, his own misery erupted like an abscess and poisoned our relationship. It became all about treading on eggshells. We measured every word and gesture because we were so afraid of the other's reaction. Eventually we said almost nothing, until there was nothing left to say."

Cherry reached out and touched Magda's hand. Magda felt her friend's heart pumping new blood into her soul, reviving her at last.

★

Magda had the make-up samples ready for the seventh week. The little pots of thick colour would be the seal on their friendship. She wouldn't charge Cherry for these. She had never had a true friend until now. Generosity was a natural consequence of friendship. A bottle of sparkling wine was chilling in the fridge so they could toast the concealment of the stain.

"Magda, I think I'm making real progress," Cherry said as she sat down. "I'm incredibly thrilled. I was asked to speak out of the blue yesterday. A colleague fell ill and I was given her notes. Maybe it was the short notice and my feathers didn't have time to get ruffled. Maybe the notes seemed less personal, less emotive, as they weren't mine. But, whatever the reason, I stood there in my actress pose, just as you taught me, and delivered it almost without a stumble. Loud, clear and word-perfect!" Cherry beamed.

"But it's too soon," Magda said, frowning. "We haven't finished our sessions. You're not ready."

"Well, I'm not quite there yet, I don't suppose, because if the session had been longer or if there had been questions afterwards, I'm not sure I'd have coped. I was beginning to crumble. The last sentence or two were quite shaky, I suppose. And I sat down much too quickly with sheer relief!"

"It's a shame you didn't pass the responsibility on to someone else, Cherry. I haven't completed you yet. Today's session is the vital one."

Cherry's harvest-moon face deflated a little. She looked stricken. "Oh, Magda, I'm so sorry. I felt so much better, you see. And that's all thanks to you for giving me so much confidence. Now I've disappointed you, haven't I?"

Magda's moment had arrived at last. "Well Cherry, there's really no problem at all in this instance. I can swallow the disappointment because I'm so excited tonight! Now, over there on the sideboard

24

are some gifts for you. Extra-special cosmetics. Your best secret weapon yet." Magda was smiling with the foretaste of Cherry's joy. "I'll help you apply them at first, then let you see in the mirror."

An unnatural silence overwhelmed the room like a sudden darkness, as if a bulb had blown, casting a strange shadow.

Magda couldn't find her voice in this drab mood that was bleeding through the carpet, seeping up the walls, leaching into the ceiling. She knew there would be no way of turning things back to how they were.

Finally, her voice sounding injured, Cherry cleared her throat to speak. "Is this what you think I need?"

"Well, I think of it as the icing on the cake, really, Cherry," Magda said with forced brightness, relieved she had found such a neat summary. This might work. Yes, she was sure it would. Cherry would recover her normal exuberance. "Do give it a try and you'll be thrilled. I know you will."

Cherry picked up a pot and her face was so serious, so crestfallen, that she wasn't Cherry any more. The pot dangled from her fingers. She put it down again without a sound and stared at it.

"Cherry, I'm not judging you by your birthmark," Magda said. "It's not a problem at all. But others might be swayed by it. They might see it before they see you, that's all."

"I have never felt judged, Magda," Cherry said, gripping the edge of the sideboard. "It hasn't ever occurred to me that I should wear a mask. If people do stare for a moment, I can understand that. But I always thought I had a cheerful enough personality that would shine through."

Magda released the breath she had held while Cherry spoke. "Oh, of course you have, Cherry. You really sparkle. That is such an advantage. It wouldn't do at all to be a shrinking violet in your shoes. You are so right."

Cherry looked up from the sideboard, straight into Magda's eyes. "In *my* shoes, Magda?"

"Well yes. I mean, it always pays to retain a good humour when one has some kind of disfigurement. One puts a brave face on for the world, so to speak."

"A brave face?"

"Yes and you do it so well, Cherry," Magda trilled, delighted with how this was going. "Your courage has made me stronger too. When I think of how you must have suffered. I mean, the rest of the world can seem so perfect and that makes our own flaws feel more obvious than they are. Makes us feel worthless."

"I've never thought having a simple birthmark was the same as being worthless," Cherry said, her tone flat. "Is that how you think, Magda?"

"Oh no, no. Of course not. But it could be an impediment. People staring. Or turning away." Magda knew she sounded desperate.

"No one has ever turned away from me," Cherry said in the same formal voice. "I think of my mark as intriguing, unique. And I thought others felt the same. I was brought up to be positive about it. It's livid and large and exceptional, yes. But I didn't think it was a repulsive thing."

"It's not that noticeable, Cherry, really it isn't!" Magda said, feeling the floor turning to eggshells again, as if she had whirled back to those last terrible days with Kevin, their grief held by the tips of their fingernails like a glass egg between them while they glided apart.

"It most certainly is, Magda," Cherry said. "It's extremely noticeable."

"I've seen worse."

"I doubt it." Cherry turned to Magda, as the sun flared for the final time, glinting like a flame on her locket before it sank at last. "But I truly thought it didn't hold me back. And I thought you were giving me the confidence I lacked at public speaking. I was so happy because I thought you were working on that. I had no notion at all that you were simply building up to a makeover."

"I wanted to help, I..."

"The sincerity of our relationship was something I cherished, Magda. I thought you were a friend."

"I am, Cherry, I am."

"I'll send the money for these," Cherry said, indicating the row of pots with a brisk wave of her hand. She picked up her bag and left, leaving a waft of her beautiful perfume as she closed the door.

★

Months later, walking alone by the harbour, Magda happened to see Alison Smedley.

"Oh, Magda, you should see how Cherry Marshall's blossoming. The baby's almost due and she's so thrilled with her new home. The nursery's pale yellow. A sort of sophisticated banana-custard."

"I didn't know she..."

"Yes, she's really excited. They're holding the job for her, but I think motherhood will keep her at home. She's made for it, isn't she? So full of warmth, so nurturing. And her husband's an angel. Doesn't let her out of his sight. Makes her put her feet up. They're the perfect pair, really."

"She never said..."

"Well, maybe she thought it wouldn't be professional to talk about herself. She was just your client after all. Cherry's very thoughtful. Wouldn't have wasted your time with chit-chat. Sensitive to things like that, is our Cherry."

Before Last Wednesday

Valerie was polishing the ashtray at dawn. Tiny musical sounds. The huff of her breath, the squeak of the duster on the moistened onyx. She skimmed the ashtray towards the matching cigarette lighter on the glass coffee table, until they were almost touching. She added the brick of slim mints. No. Too contrived. She separated them, retaining their proportionate distance, relishing their reflections.

She patted the cushions of the Parker Knoll. Four days before he told her the terrible news, Simon had sat there with a pin, spearing his Saturday winkles. Now the chair was waiting for Mr Gosling. She felt at odds with it, like watching someone else's dream.

She swished the sweeper in careful cadence. Too fast and stray flecks would flip into the air. She massaged the sun-bleached paperback spines with her duster, angling her neck to study the beloved titles: *Secret Passion. Unbridled Bliss.*

She sat by the cocktail cabinet and considered the liqueur glasses. Thin and etched with a pattern reminiscent of swastikas, they were far too fragile to use. But Mr Gosling might want a Benedictine. She rubbed at the neck of the sticky bottle.

There was lemonade in the fridge for the girl. Would she eat the cheese-straws that were filling the house with hot pastry steam?

Valerie checked the cooling-rack in the kitchen. Fifteen cheese straws. Adele might hand them round to everyone if she was in her obliging mood.

When Valerie returned to the lounge with her can of perfumed air, Adele was looking out of the window at the sea.

"Oh, you're up, dear. I've already rolled out the pastry. Couldn't sleep. I saved some scraps for you."

Adele raised her deep-bored eyes to a gull tugged askew by the gale.

"You could cut out some tarts."

Valerie recalled the name of the girl for whom Simon had brought home the lemonade, making full use of his manager's ten per cent discount. Emma. It was a pretty name. Seventeen. An age for dipping into cosmetics, dabbing on cologne and gazing with a pout at one's reflection in shop windows. An age for casting sooty-lashed eyes at men in fawn trousers.

Adele was seventeen too. As tall as her father and broader-shouldered. Hunched in a jumper zipped up to her chin, she was obstructing the early sun. Her bottle-green slacks were decayed, wilting. But she refused to wear anything fresher. Incipient spots mildewed her forehead. She was watching a twisted carrier-bag spin cartwheels along the sand. Her long shoes pointed straight ahead to the horizon.

The bannister creaked. It sounded like a wounded dog. Valerie frowned. Simon ought to fix those spindles. Teak shouldn't yelp like that. Slippers shuffled on the hall tiles. That meant he was in his dressing-gown. She thought he would be dressed; shoes on ready for Adele's walk. The poor child wouldn't be calm if she missed it. The dog swept his tail back and forth on the carpet, sculpting a crescent moon into the pile.

Simon was unshaven and pale. He put an arm across Adele's shoulders.

"We'll go for a walk soon. Don't get all agitated now, will you?

Good job you haven't got a tail, isn't it? Look at Ned swatting the table leg with his. Look, Adele!"

Adele rasped her usual three barks of laughter. The Venetian blinds quivered in the draught and slipped askew, unfolding on top of Valerie's porcelain village.

Simon had old boiled egg-yolk on his pyjama collar. He didn't look much like a Grade Seven supermarket manager who'd been twice to Majorca. Valerie thought he looked like a grubby old man who had been caught with his trousers round his ankles. A man whose eyes didn't meet hers when she spoke.

"Will you be ready by eleven?"

"Yes, yes. But do we have to fuss, Valerie?"

"I'd like things to be nice, Simon."

"Where will we put Adele?"

"Put?"

"Well, she won't understand, will she? She'll stroke Emma's hair and be...oh, I don't know." He was flushing and there were black patches under his arms. He pulled at his dressing-gown cord until it cut into his paunch.

"Oh, does she have long hair?" Valerie asked, flinching at the mention of Emma's name. She had always been 'the new till-girl' until last Wednesday.

Simon didn't answer, but he looked irritated, as if she were a child asking pointless questions.

"Adele will want to help," Valerie said. "She'll think it's a party, like the house-warming."

"Christ, you're not getting the bloody fondue out, are you?"

Valerie smoothed her trousers and went to the hall mirror to crisp her hair with spray.

Simon trailed out to find her, Adele attached to his sleeve, a thumb in her mouth.

"Sorry, Val. You know I'm not comfortable with this. I'll dress quickly and take Adele to the beach with Ned."

Valerie went upstairs too. While Simon was shaving, she made the twin beds in their room, walking between them to check the gap was the usual body's width.

In Adele's room she drew back the curtains and arranged the dolls in a row on the eiderdown, where they stared at the new day. She draped the old christening dress over the Woolworth baby's bitten plastic toes. Its painted eyebrows arched with curiosity. Its parted lips smirked. She pierced the mouth-hole with its dummy.

In the lounge, the air hung heavy with sweet-peas and fresh pastry. Simon and Adele took Ned out into the clean air. Valerie flipped Mantovani out of his sleeve and onto the stereo. She felt shaky. The music would be a distraction. She'd have to watch it, though. Adele would be back soon and 'Trolley Song' got her all flustered. It was the *ding-ding* bit. Track Seven.

It was a shame they hadn't had the suite re-covered yet. Never mind, it was quite a nice nutmeg shade, except for the bald patch where Ned always lay. She could put Simon there. Adele was best standing up. Otherwise she was inclined to break wind into the cushions.

It was close to eleven. Valerie waited at the window with a cigarette, puckering her mouth like a trumpeter to save her lipstick.

There they were. Simon was all windswept. He would have to comb his hair back over. Adele was lumbering along with her arms full of shells.

As they waved at Valerie from the path, she felt sick with longing for their life before last Wednesday. Simon had held her hand across the space between the beds and told her about the baby coming.

Valerie thought he was just telling her snippets of faraway news from work. Reg Wilson's bought a Datsun Cherry. Marge Curtis has tried the new restaurant with the plastic Tudor beams and said the redcurrant cheesecake was far too rich. Oh, and...er...the new till-girl's having my baby.

A red car pulled up. Valerie pinched out her cigarette, tucked it in her apron pocket. Simon was looking at her with desperation. The wind whipped his hair across his eyes like a mask of shame.

"Better get in," she mouthed through the glass. He tucked himself behind her in the hall like a schoolboy waiting outside the headmaster's door. Adele took her shells round to the back garden to wash them with the hose.

Home didn't seem like home. Valerie felt as if she might be rehearsing a role for *Play for Today*. Wife greeting Visitors. Or Amiable Housewife in a commercial for the cheesy puffs she was handing round or for the Hostess trolley Simon had bought her last Thursday.

Mr Gosling wouldn't sit down. He stayed by the window and glanced out at his car, hands on hips and lips pressed into a gash across his face. After a minute, he took off his trilby and sat it by the cocktail onions. He refused a drink, but shot out an arm and pointed at Emma, who perched on the edge of the sofa as if he had instructed her in the car not to interfere.

"This is my daughter." He looked down quickly and studied the carpet.

Simon said nothing. He showed a similar interest in the cream shag-pile. The introduction was fruitless and somehow shaming, since it was clear he already knew this girl beneath her clothes.

Emma and Valerie said 'Hello' at the same time. Valerie had expected a blonde with bitty nail varnish and a shelf of bust jutting from her pale-pink supermarket uniform, not this rabbity girl draped in a grey mac, ears protruding from oily hair. She looked more like a Deirdre than an Emma.

The silence was saved by Mantovani's cascading strings. As Simon padded to the vinyl chair beside the sofa, the golden horns struck up and he was forced to move in reluctant time to their rhythm.

Valerie's little finger scratched the stray grains of lipstick from the corners of her mouth.

"Salmon bap, Mr Gosling?"

"No thanks."

"It's boneless."

"Look. I can see you've done all this," he said, thrusting his solid arm towards the nibbles. "But I'm here for Emma. She's seventeen." He said the word syllable by syllable, his saliva peppering the salted nuts. "Se-ven-teen, for God's sake. And you... you are an old man, old enough to be her father. Maybe her grandfather even."

Simon hung his head like a man trapped in the hearth of Hell. That was how he'd looked when the doctors said Adele was a walking vegetable. All his pomp gone.

Whenever Valerie saw Simon in his supermarket, he swaggered along the aisles, one finger rolling rogue tins round to face front or pointing old ladies at the custard-powder. It was like watching a pageant. He walked with a kind of strut, his flared trousers flapping. Now, he was just a silly man in a cardigan. And a finger was pointing at him.

"Look, as far as I see it," Mr Gosling said, placing himself in front of the living-flame fireplace, "we have two choices here. Either he gets divorced and marries my daughter sharpish, or he pays cash for his pleasure and stays away."

Pleased with his speech, he rocked on his feet and folded his arms, as though he had trussed up a meaty business deal. Valerie pulled the trolley towards her like a shield. He talked about her and Simon as though they had no finer feelings at all. And he had very girlish hands. She glanced at the vol-au-vents. They'd heat up nicely for tea later.

Bullets of water rained on the patio doors at the other end of the long room. Adele had abandoned the hose. It stood erect and spinning, while she squatted under the lilac bush with her knickers round her ankles. Valerie glided down the length of the room, shimmied through the narrow gap between the dining table and sideboard and closed the blinds.

33

"Sun's a bit bright," she said as she sat on the arm of Simon's chair and handed him a cigarette.

Emma was pressing her tongue inside her drained liqueur glass. Valerie could see the mound of pink cotton frock where the girl's mac gaped. It seemed separate, almost quivering with its own pulse like the raspberry blancmange rabbit she had made for Adele's birthday.

It came home to Valerie then. This was nothing to do with buck-toothed foolish girls or vain little men. This was someone pure emerging from a furtive grope on the stockroom floor. This was the brand-new child she and Simon had waited for seventeen years ago. A baby they could love. By some silly mishap, some miscalculation that could be dismissed and forgotten, this girl happened to be carrying their child.

"What are your plans? What are you hoping for?" Valerie asked, leaning towards Emma, blocking the girl's father. He could remain backstage now, his lines delivered.

"Who me?" Emma giggled and chewed a fingernail. "Don't know really. Um, I can't wait to get back into normal clothes. Yeah, I think that's what I'm excited about really."

Valerie refilled Emma's glass. "Getting back to normal, yes. I imagine that's going to be important for you, dear. Gherkin?"

"Mmm. My boyfriend hates me like this." She poked at her dress.

"Well, babies turn your life upside down even more than pregnancy does, I'm afraid."

"Mmm, especially if they're ugly. A girl at my school had one that looked like a toad. One that had been squashed on the road."

"It's the disturbed sleep and the washing I was..."

"And my boyfriend hates my black nipples."

Mr Gosling paced on the hearthrug, then balanced on the fender to gain more height. "I just can't see her marrying a divorced chap. Won't have it. She needs cash. More space in the house. I've planned a lean-to. My brother-in-law's an architect, as it happens."

He paused and rocked more rapidly. "She can marry her boyfriend. We've got time to squeeze in a small wedding. No fuss."

Valerie expected him to say he had a cousin who was a vicar, or a niece that did flowers. He was shaping Emma's life just as surely as he had helped to create it seventeen years ago. He was guiding her over a hurdle just as he would have once swung her into the air and over a puddle.

She went to Emma and sat close beside her. "We'll have the baby, dear. We've got a spare room doing nothing. I'll show it to you. Then you can carry on as if this never happened."

"All right then. I'll just take some cash." Emma held out her glass as Adele lumbered into the lounge. 'Trolley Song' was reaching its climax. The stylus faltered on a scratch in the vinyl. There was a piercing squeal.

Adele writhed to the repetition of the ringing bell, tearing at her clothes. She lunged at Emma's hair, raking it with rough fingers. Cheese straws littered the carpet and the swastika glass smashed into a million glittering specks.

Mr Gosling left the fender, cannoned off the Hostess and grasped his daughter. "Bloody madhouse, this is. Come on, Emma."

"Help me up, Dad, and get this nutter off me. God, I'd rather give the kid to a Home than leave it here, thanks. It's not decent. She hasn't even got any bloody knickers on."

When they left, Mr Gosling banged the front-door with such ferocity the glass panel trembled.

Simon stroked his daughter's back to soothe her while Valerie lifted the stylus from Track Seven and returned it to its clip. Adele liked the Hoover, so Valerie vacuumed while Simon cradled their child in his arms.

They all carried the food to the beach and Valerie spread out the picnic. Whenever one of them shifted position, a little pocket of sand opened up and they watched a Tupperware tub sink deeper and deeper until it was quite embedded.

The afternoon faded and another bout of drizzle drove them home. Simon helped Adele organise her flannel and toothbrush. She was exhausted. He promised to read her a story before she went to sleep.

Valerie was tired too, but she went to the bathroom to roll up her hair. Simon came in to floss. She watched his reflection, his hands sawing the string. He watched hers, mouth open in concentration as she pushed the pins firmly home. Valerie went to their bedroom first and sighed without a sound, as she folded back the eiderdowns and pushed the twin beds together.

DECISIONS MADE OVER
MADELEINE'S TOAST

One by one, Andrew unfolded Stephanie's fingers from the sugar dispenser and tipped it once, twice, into his cup. There was not enough. Spilt grains winked from the table while he went to find a teaspoon. The woman who served at the counter was grumbling to the manager. He was hidden behind a steam-withered curtain.

"This toaster keeps jamming, Si. And it's chucking out smoke something chronic."

"Dragon then, ain't it? Like you, Madeleine." He peered out from his den and grinned at Stephanie, pleased with his answer.

Stephanie stared at the strip light tube reflected on her coffee and touched the hospital band around her wrist. Her name was bleeding under its plastic cover.

Andrew came back to the table, twirling the spoon and humming. Stephanie couldn't work out the tune. It was just another sound, like Madeleine's knife spearing the innards of the toaster.

Andrew wanted things to be normal again, she could tell. He welcomed all noises, glancing up with interest at the slightest movement; a customer scraping a chair or Madeleine scraping toast. He fidgeted in his seat and looked around with satisfaction, as if they were sitting in the Ritz with a piano tinkling or on the deck of a cruise ship weaving around tropical islands.

Madeleine. It was a nice name. It didn't suit the woman with her cadaverous face and beehive of stiff hair. She looked like an axe-head wearing a crash helmet.

Stephanie watched Andrew stir his tea and study the menu he already knew. How could he be so ordinary? His eyes paused at double eggs on a fried slice. He flicked a glance at her. She knew she was frightening him.

He looked across at an open-mouthed model discarded on the next table. She was lying on a leopard rug, her long hair draped around her. A taxi driver breezed in and claimed her. After a few desperate gulps of morning tea, he folded her with a satisfied sigh and slid her into his pocket. Stephanie wondered if Andrew was wishing he could change places with the taxi driver and go out of this clammy heat and toast-smoke into the day. Or maybe he was wishing he could be folded up and hidden in someone's pocket.

Andrew tapped a bored foot, as if he thought being ordinary might be a remedy.

It was Wednesday. Would he go to The Lamb later with the lads? And even though it was only nine in the morning and she was just out of hospital, he was already wearing his snooker jeans and the red polo top that clashed with his ginger hair. She could see the outline of his lucky cube of blue chalk in the breast-pocket.

She couldn't ask him to skip it, but if he chose to stay in tonight and made her that awful coffee he did with boiling milk, it could turn into a sad, but special sort of ordinary. It would be coffee made with boiling love. Not ordinary at all.

Stretching across the table, he stroked her cheek. The softness of his fingers made her gasp.

"Actually, it's probably best if we don't stop to eat, Steph," he said. "Got loads on today."

His feet shuffled, pushing her overnight bag underneath the table. The plastic handle-loops sweated between their legs. He had dropped the bag down like holiday luggage, like the doctors dropped their baby in a dish.

"Just a round of toast, then? Or not bother?" he said.

She didn't know. Toast was a compromise between a meal and nothing at all. In between. Something that was better than nothing.

She couldn't answer because she didn't know what he wanted her to say.

He sighed and went to the counter to wait for Madeleine to notice, his calf muscles twitching in his jeans and his hand jingling coins in his right pocket.

The toast arrived, drowning in butter.

"I don't like butter, remember?" Stephanie said.

Andrew went back and held it out to Madeleine. "She didn't ask for butter," he said, passing her the plate.

Madeleine's face was granite. She slapped the plate down, the butter glaring under the unforgiving light until it sank in.

"You'll have to wait," she said, motioning him back to the table.

The long hand of the huge café clock struggled to the next minute. Andrew rasped his chair back, letting it tip until it balanced on two legs. He had to stretch forward to drum his spoon on the table's edge.

"You should eat butter, Steph. Mum said you look like a wafer these days."

"I haven't been to yours for ages, though."

"She saw you in town buying that nightie, or whatever, for the hospital. She didn't bother saying hello."

"Why not?"

"Said you looked a bit miserable. Like you didn't want to talk to no one."

"Does she know about...?"

"Nah. It's done with. Pointless having her go on about it."

Their child was done with. The doctor with flat hands and spearmint-breath had called it a Procedure. And the Procedure was over. Done with. Don't worry.

She couldn't look at Andrew, but she knew he was looking at her. Was he thinking about later? Would he call off the snooker?

One inch long it was now. Or had been.

"Do you remember falling off that wooden horse in the park that time?" she asked him. "It was in that kids' playground. A little horse on a giant spring that buckled under you. Remember? That day we went for a walk in the snow and no one was there? And you just splatted into the snow and we couldn't stop laughing."

"Nah. Sorry."

She bit her lip, cross with herself. She should have known he didn't keep a stack of memories in his head. Things just came and went for some people.

"Oh, yeah," he said, nodding too much. "I think I might do, now. Yeah." He reached across to another table and took an abandoned newspaper. He read out the crossword puzzle clues, but Stephanie's answers wouldn't fit into the blank little squares. She heard him sigh.

The new toast came, black on one side.

"Gonna eat that?"

"It's a bit burnt. Look at the underneath side."

"Be all right. Bit of jam, look."

He went to Madeleine and came back with a chocolate biscuit in cellophane. He looked pleased with himself.

"Sugar for shock, so my Gran says," he said, skidding the biscuit across the table to her. It stuck to a greasy mark on the melamine.

"It wasn't a shock though, was it?" she said. "We chose."

And Andrew was choosing for their lives to go back to being the same. Back to bacon for breakfast instead of throwing up. No more staring at walls.

He wasn't answering her. His patience was thinner these days. Like a sucked barley-sugar. Brittle, transparent. Ready to shatter.

"Can't you learn when to leave well alone, Steph?"

He stood up. His chair scuffed the floor and made Madeleine look up with a scowl. He gathered his things, sticky from the table. He knew his next move. There was an elegance about him that Stephanie envied.

In the corner, a workman wearing a donkey-jacket was jabbing at sausages, swilling half-chewed mouthfuls down with tea. Speed-eating, clock-watching. His lift arrived before he had finished.

The old couple by the window gathered their slack shopping bags from the spare seat, their tea-cake crusts discarded on the plates. Sucking crumbs from their teeth, they left to catch the nine-fifteen bus waiting outside the café. They had not spoken to one another, but Stephanie saw how he helped her onto the bus, holding her arm as if it were porcelain.

She saw Madeleine timing Si's tea-break, her next cigarette lying with her lighter on top of the packet, primed for her own break in the fresh air by the dustbins.

Everyone had a next move that depended on someone else.

Andrew's long fingers curled round his wallet, keys and chewing gum. After a moment's consideration, he picked up the biscuit. She saw the pad of his thumb make an imprint on the wrapper and wondered how he could fit so many things into one hand.

He dropped the things back on the table. Stephanie's head shot up. She waited for him to tell her what to do. He was reaching into the inside pocket of his jacket.

Rain lunged at the windows. Madeleine was draped across the *Daily Mail*. Si hurried in and perched by the unlit fruit machine, the remains of his bacon sandwich dripping tomato sauce onto the floor. The untuned radio fizzed. Edges of forgotten toast curled up.

"Ah, there it is," Andrew said, opening a velvet box. He nestled it in his palm, shaped his hand around it and opened the lid. He unravelled a gold bracelet with ornate, twisted links. A gold heart swung from it.

"Not bad, is it? I'm taking it to the engravers. It's gonna say, *For Grace, a beloved mother.* Better shoot off actually. Get it sorted. It's Mum's birthday Friday."

Grace. Stephanie liked that name too.

Andrew palmed everything for the last time. He checked his pockets, clapping them for reassurance that he had picked up all his belongings. But Stephanie knew he could see without doubt that nothing was left behind.

"Want my toast?" he asked. "I'll leave it for you. Do you good to sit here for a bit. It's raining hard."

They looked at the darkening windows.

"Don't you want me to come with you?" she asked as he turned away.

A shower of hail hammered down. Everyone in the café turned to the window, as if this were a spectacle staged for their collective benefit. But the hail didn't last. In a few seconds it was over and done with.

Andrew shuffled the zip of his jacket up and down. The Saint Christopher she'd given him glinted on his chest. She was glad it didn't rest in a tangle of hair, glad it shone out on his smooth skin.

Christopher. A good name.

Stephanie looked up at Andrew's beautiful lips moving while he grated the zip up and down, up and down. Madeleine was flapping a tea towel at the toaster. Life throbbed back into the fruit machine. Rain rattled down in short bursts, half-hearted now. And amid all the rasping, flapping, throbbing and rattling, Andrew was leaving her.

"Are you listening, Steph? I'm saying we need a bit of space. It's been hard for me. I feel like I've been to hell with all this.

42

You're so bloody moody these days. I'm gonna stay at Mum's. I took my stuff back there last night while you were sleeping it off at the hospital. I'll give you a ring sometime. Let the dust settle."

A ring. He had given her a ring once. From a cracker. Bendy red plastic. Full of Christmas wine, he had pushed it onto her finger.

The sun was breaking through, revealing all the sugar crystals scattered on the table.

"I can still smell the hospital," Stephanie told Andrew.

But he was zipping right up to the neck now and reminding her to pick up her bag when she went. He spoke to Madeleine on his way out and thudded a few coins onto her *Daily Mail*. She brought another round of toast to Stephanie. It was underdone this time, like two slices of beige fleece.

"Bloody toaster's a waste of space," Madeleine shouted to Si.

"Like you then!" he barked back. "Always bloody something, ain't it, eh? It was the fryer last week. It'll be the kettle next. Talking of which, I'm gasping. Make us another cuppa, love. Please. Bloody nectar, your tea is."

Madeleine patted her bee-hive and smiled at him. He winked back and she kept on patting and smiling.

Stephanie wondered why toast came in rounds when bread was square. She looked at the plate and saw a kidney-shaped metal bowl. She looked at a bleached poster of a girl in a bikini holding a giant pork pie. Sliced in half, pink and mottled.

A young mother came in, dragging a child called Thomas. *Thomas.* A nice name.

Thomas shouted and kicked his mother's leg, raging at the day.

"Will you sodding well be quiet," the mother roared.

Thomas, tear-drenched, staggered past Stephanie's table.

"If you don't come here, my lad," the mother yelled, "you'll wish you'd never been born."

Stephanie shredded a serviette over the toast. Tears were

swelling in her eyes, but she mustn't blink. Mustn't let them fall. Madeleine was staring at her.

She knew she was going to hear lots of words that didn't mean anything. Not unless she let them.

Andrew had probably spoken without thinking too. He was upset. It wasn't just women who felt bad about things like this. Men could get in a state. They just showed it in a different way. And it was kind of him to get the bracelet for his mum. It showed he was thoughtful, didn't it? Even at a time like this.

The café was filling with hungry people bagging their favourite tables, sheltering from the rain. They would move on. Another bus would arrive, spilling people out and sucking people in.

Stephanie propped the menu against the vinegar bottle. With her foot she pushed her bag out from under the table. The café was swimming, watery like a tired rainbow. Bloody tears. Why wouldn't they just dry up?

The nine-thirty arrived, hissing through the long puddle that had collected while she sat in the café. It would take her somewhere. She could ask the conductor. In fact, it might be the bus that stopped really close to Andrew's mum's. She stood up.

Or she could wait here, sipping bad tea. Hearing names that meant nothing. Watching people come and go.

She pulled off the wristband, twisted it and left it with the destroyed serviette. She pushed the plate to the edge of the table. The toast had not been made with much love.

WIND AND WATER

I said to Pa how, if the invisible man posted a letter into Mercy's Mercantile today, he'd be seen for sure. Every tractor is idle. Every cow lowin' to be milked. Every man searchin'. Every woman waitin' at a window. The school won't open save for search parties to gather.

My feet slap across the flat land by the sea, through the salicornia a-growin' in the salt, whipping at my legs in the wind. It looks like fire when it turns red. A sea of fire makes no sense, but it sure does look that way. I'm walkin' through wet flame. The plant has the tiniest leaves, but until you're close up you'd think it was just grass.

The letter in my pocket stings my leg under my shorts. Pa says to post it into the shop when there's no one around. I have to look over my shoulders, twice or thrice times, turn right around and then act like I'm just havin' a regular play with a good pebble from the grass, clangin' it against the shop.

We're always smashing stones at the corrugated iron. We don't make marks. Just noise. Only for jestin', not for people to spin right around and stare. I turned eighteen in the summer, so I guess throwing stones oughta belong to some other time. Mighty glad I got one last chance.

I wish Caleb was here with me. He's so dumb he makes me braver. Crackpot, is what Pa calls it. Caleb wouldn't know how to post a letter without anyone seein'. There's a lot of movement when you post a letter. Think of all you do. You stop. You squat if the slot is way down near the kickboard.

You near enough need to lie on your belly to slide anything into the shop's slot. Then you have to pull your hand free of the flap before it snaps you like a fly-trap from Venus. In winter-gloves it takes time.

I ain't done it yet. I'm a-thinkin' about it first. And that's what Caleb can't do. Think. I'm looking close. Same as eyeing up the breadth of a leap from the sea-fence so you don't git yourself caught in the mire. You guess the direction your pebble will take, make sure it hits the metal, not the pane that's too darn smeared for me to call it a window.

Pa said to use cunning and daring. He said life's a waste if you don't. No one can learn them to you at school. He's dependin' on me, he says. He tells me to look deep in his eyes and see the truth. And the only truth I need to know is that I'm loved.

Pa's the only living soul I got. And family is the salt of the earth. You stay with what you have, even if there's just the one. And he's grey-grizzled and creaking. No matter. You stay where you're loved.

Pa drove the tractor when he was blind drunk. He drove it off furrow. He drove it where a barrow of frozen earth marked my sister's grave. Tractor caught the edge of the barrow. It ploughed through Ma on account of she was grievin' there.

She was tired. She never heard it comin' at her through the dark. By the time she felt the thunder of it in the earth, it was too damn late.

She was my mother and she was lame. She dropped to the ground because there weren't nowhere else. She was tired and lame, my mother. The wheel that's taller than me rolled over her head.

The trial's soon. But they didn't clap him in jail. They know he's going nowhere. They watch him, but he's just an old man in mourning. And they know he won't leave me.

Caleb's ma and pa say when Pa's locked away, they'll sop me up like suckin' an oyster from its shell. There's thirteen boys and girls in that family at the last count. Just the one bed for the menfolk. But I ain't gonna be tellin' my private business in my sleep. No way, Pa tells me. It won't happen.

Wish I was walking with Caleb right now. There's everyone out here calling him and whacking the marshes with sticks, but I'm alone. I wait. My breath comes out so hard I can see it.

A heron watching a tide pool is also watching me. He lives in the creek, waiting for fish to leak out from the marsh when the tide changes. Mummichogs and grass-shrimp crouch in a pool of marsh water for the tide to go out. A diamondback terrapin is laying its eggs, one eye turned toward me. Alligators are basking behind me in fresher brine. Their heads turn at every move I make. Even just a sigh.

If I walk to the shop like any other day and post the letter as if it's the most regular thing in the world anyone can do, no one will notice. No stealth. Just walk up brisk, quick look over the shoulders, thrice times, and bam. Done.

The shop's doing business today. Fifty folk could go missing round here and still Mercy's Mercantile would be open for the world and his wife to see her fat old dugs leanin' squat on the counter.

Mind you, she's kept the door closed today and slapped the flimsy screen over it. Ain't no flies at this time of year, but Mercy wishes to show respect for the family of a missing boy. A kind of mourning. Everyone knows that a missing person round here is oft-times never seen again. Lost to the marsh, crusted with salt way down where the small fishes bite all day and all night.

Mercy, she misses nothing. But today, with the screen across, she only has the window. And it ain't seen a leather for months. If I creep from the back and round the side, I can throw myself to the ground, push the letter through the darned slot and be gone. She might think the wind had just high-whistled, the way it does, squealin' right around her steel shack of a shop. And I can hear her saying, "My, I hope Caleb has a coat about his back if he's hunkered out in this all night long." And I can see her take a draw on her cigarillo and tug at her bodice to ease the strain while she leans and waits and catches sight of the letter we made from a paper-bag, a white square on her floor.

I don't know why I want Caleb here. He's a wretch, the worst coward I know. Pa says we can put our hands in Caleb's mind like we dip them in the dish-water, scootin' things about, swirlin' and swishin', gittin' the stuck dirt off and bringin' them out clean. And Caleb would scarce notice.

When you're alone, anyone counts, but Caleb sure would mess this up if he stood beside me now. He'd wet hisself like he does in the night. Wind and water, that's what Caleb is. Wind and water. Like this place, only without its silent suckin' strength. Without its hidden eyes, its hidden heart.

Anyways, if Caleb was here, he wouldn't be where he is now.

The search is sterner. Hands and arms sweep trees aside. Shouts and barks circle in the wind. But the hope folk had at the git-go is flagging. Caleb is slow, people are sayin'. He could be anywhere under that great sky full of milk up there. Or he could be way below the foggy water that waits to take a soul down. I see them look up. And I see them look down. That's how's I know what folks are sayin'.

Pa's hands are busy now. I can feel it. I'm a thousand paces from our house, but I know it. I stride to the shop. I can feel Mercy's hands itchin' for me to come by. They paw me in back of the shop when I bring her the marrows. Pa and I grow them, great shining fruits of the soil. And yams with their dirt-jackets. Cut them and warm yourself on the glow.

I bring them for her to sell in the shop and she goes roamin' all over me. "Fresh from the earth today, Miss Mercy," I tell her, "and that's not me I'm talkin' about, mind. Just check out what I got in my sack, Miss Mercy."

She laughs some. She don't give over for a full minute. And still she touches me. Means nothing by it. Loveless place, her shop, she says. Says she has to git it where she can.

Three glances over my shoulder and I'm down. I push the letter in. I think Pa knows it's there. I can feel him unstrapping the ties, peeling off the gag. And there's Caleb with the words scrambling in his head. We just have to hope they come out the right way. Pa reckons the only way to get truth out is to put truth in.

My scarf made the gag. Pa took it off to give him his grits. We let the butter melt right in. That's the way Caleb eats it if he ever gits the chance. He said he'd pray to the good Lord to stay right there, bound though he was, just for those grits.

He smiled in our chair with the strips of flannel and sheet gripping his wrists and ankles hard. His brain only knows about right now. The past only stays in his head for the beat of a bunting's wing.

Pa told him again how things were that day. Caleb nodded away, butter grooving on down his chin and collecting in the stupid dimple he's got there. He will say the right thing.

I walk around the shop the other way. The wind and I glide together, unchecked. No one's here. Mercy is humming inside, clattering open the jar of chewin'-nuts that have cost her all but three teeth. The counter creaks under her weight.

People say she's Caleb's true mother. She lived with her Grampa 'til he drank hisself to string and piss. He was nothin' but veins, they say. People round here say things all the time. They say her babe came one night after a ten-month of being inside her. Small, they said, but the head swollen like it was a creature from another place. So swollen that Mercy's scream was heard right down as far as the fresh water. A mermaid, they say, shivered on the sea-bed that night.

No one counts the folk at Caleb's. No one does a reckoning-up of how much love's left in his mother's heart. She takes in anyone lost. In that bed that slants and dips, the bed where Caleb and all the rest sleep, who knows which belong by blood? Caleb's mother loves them all. They're all hers.

By now, Mercy will be seeing the letter. As I walk away to the marsh, she is picking it up, her breath coming hard as she stoops. Her old stays crackle as she lets out a sigh.

I stand still, let the crows settle, wait for the air to clear. And I swear I hear her unfold the paper and run her finger under the words. Might take her some time. The nuts might have to sit on her tongue while her mouth gapes like a flounder at what she's reading.

I'll hear her scream. And if I wait long enough, I'll hear the whistles and the shouts that awaken the search for Caleb.

I'm hidin' 'cause I'm fearin' of the truth, was what he wrote. *And the sea must surely take me. It can darn well wash my shame clean away.*

He wrote the words hisself. His hand shook enough to scramble a cackleberry, on account of he was scared black of the face of truth.

Aren't all of us damn scared of it? I sure am scared of what'll happen to Caleb now. He drove a tractor that don't belong to him and mowed down an innocent woman prayin' at the graveside. He let folk think Pa was at the wheel. He got Pa to save his damn hide. Until now.

★

I watched Pa outside at night, not sleeping, while he mourned his wife, just as if he'd been halved under that wheel too. Not sleeping 'cause he feared dying in a jail cell. And I wasn't havin' it. I was havin' the truth, I told him one night when the sky turned into an old web fallin' down and the sea-pie birds had given over smashing shells for the day.

We watched an oyster reef turn silver under the moon. I could hear it rock in the swell. The water stirred. The oyster shells clicked together, a gentle clashing that made a home for barnacles and hook-mussels.

That reef had made the sea between tides a huge old hide-out for those little creatures. They gripped the oysters and nestled safe in the nooks 'tween them. I could feel the suction keepin' 'em all fast and true, hidin' them from the croakers and hardheads that slithered just below the surface. Sometimes Pa and me try to catch the weakfish, but most times they live up to their name. Their mouth muscles are so damn slack, slacker and softer than Mercy's Grampa's when the bottle was pourin' itself into his throat, that the hook rips clean out soon as it catches on. We think we're near about to take one, but they wrench free every damn time.

That night, on the bank under that great sky, we listened to the fish dream. And after a time of that, I told Pa I sure wouldn't let him tell an untruth to save Caleb.

"He might own the truth if we ask him to," I said. My words dropped like godwit chicks a-drownin'. I knew no one could force him to speak out.

I felt so goddamn impatient. I wondered why Pa was waitin', just waitin' to be taken away. I felt him keep on comin' to my bedside in the night. He whispered things in my head with tears in his old voice until the sky was down and the sea was up. He churned up my head with talk of my mother until I cried hard in my pillow like no boy should.

But one night he was done talking. The plan was made. Pa was different, like he'd reached the end of a long task and was a-sittin' back, sighing with pleasure at the ease his mind was taking.

"We'd need to coax him in, feed him whisky and tie him up. Wash his brain into confessin' without no one knowin' we done it, Pa," I said, these words sliding out, already made and shaped and as strong as the green gutweed mats that smacked over the mudflats.

He nodded. He took an age to light his pipe and made those popping sounds with it in the old way he used to do, before my mother died. He sure had reached peace inside hisself. The smoke wound its way up into the trees, like it held our secret.

I knew he'd say we could do this, we could get Caleb to speak up and let an old man live in peace with his grieving heart. I knew his answer like I'd already heard it, as if the wind had whispered it into my poor lamenting head at night. I knew Caleb's jaw would loosen and the words we drummed in would roll right back out.

"We sure can do this, Jason," Pa said, puffin' his smoke right up into the sour night sky and watchin' it vanish.

★

They find Caleb by the shore. His confession, scribbled on a bag from Mercy's shop and held in Mercy's hands as they once held poor Caleb hisself when he came from her belly, sure did make Mercy scream.

She made all the searchers swarm to the sea where he was sat on a rock, a-watchin' the tide and a-waitin'. Just like we told him.

We told Caleb they'd go easy. Comin' clean was the right thing. He was a lad and he didn't have all his head. Parts were missing, we said. And the parts of it he had left didn't match up right.

He screwed up his eyes at that. It was like making apple-pie with salt 'stead of sugar, we said. And he knew they were two things that didn't go together.

"Yep," he said. "I sure am a strange old brew." He nodded with the wisdom of it all, with the brand-new dawning truth. And we said that made him different, even maybe kinda special. And that did it.

We watched him write the confession in silence, save for the pen squawking on the paper.

★

The sheriff takes him in. People bring gifts to Pa all day. For the first time we hear them all say how they knew the whole damn time he was an innocent man. They lay their pots of jelly and flagons of berry cordial on the doorstep. We stack them in the cellar, in the cool. They stand one on top of another, like a monument to the truth, a tombstone for my poor dead mother.

I hope the nights settle now. I haven't slept well since the day the tractor went off furrow.

I'll miss Caleb, but he's just a boy and they might not keep him shut away for good and all. Me, I'm eighteen. I'm a man. They'd have locked me in the dark that never ends. Left me to rot like a brown cider-apple in the long blue grass.

★

"Think of that, boy," Pa whispered in the dark all those nights. "Think of your wasted life." He kept me strapped to the bed with his belts tied hard and pressing me down flatter than a frog on the cattle road. It was merciless. I wet the sheets. It felt hot and cold both, like a sea of fire.

But it was safe. I wasn't going anywhere held down like that with Pa breathin' the new truth in my ear, a-tellin' me what Caleb did and how he took the wheel. How I kept saying no, he shouldn't.

A sea of fire makes no sense until some soul says it sure looks that way.

And Pa whispered on into the night until the truth didn't sound like the truth any more, until it was almost invisible and made of wind and water.

Big Day Out

People who *Passed On* ate Battenberg. Journeys needed cake. Tom watched Mam slice it, waiting for the miracle of pink and yellow chequerboard.

"Me have a piece, Mam?" Lily asked, her pointed chin jutting.

Tom, wiser by three years, didn't reckon she stood an earthly. "It's Granddad's favourite, Lil," he reminded her. "Isn't it, Mam?"

Mam wasn't listening.

Lily's eyebrows rumpled. She continued wrapping her baby doll in Dad's black scarf. She packed away its lace underwear under the tea-towel that served as a mattress in the turnip-crate that served as a cot.

Mam stopped slicing and stared. She keeled over the table, one hand pressed to her back.

"Oh, Jesus wept... oh, Tom, fetch Grandma, will you?" she whispered. "But no shouting. Show respect for your Granddad for God's sake."

Tom shifted in his seat by the range, where he was helping to revive a damp, new-born lamb. He wasn't sure his name should be hand-in-glove with Our Lord's. Plus, he was hoping to avoid another glimpse of the coffin in the front room.

He would rather see Granddad at the tea table. He looked a bit serious in that box. Sort of waxy like a talking-doll whose key had dropped out mid-sentence. He must be resting before his Big Day Out. Tom would rather keep busy until Granddad woke up and put his other trousers on. His stiff suit and tie smelt of cupboards, instead of Famous Grouse.

But Mam was giving Tom a pleading look. He stood up, wishing he and Granddad were about to go fishing.

Tom was four when they'd fished the first time, huddled on the cold bank with their tackle and toffees, a north-easterly whipping the wet sedge where the mill-stream met the river.

As soon as the float sank and a flash of silver soared from the water, Tom forgot the rain and wind. He could have sat there forever. Granddad clapped him on the back with such excitement the toffee flew out of Tom's mouth and into the river.

"Tom!" Mam called. "Hurry!"

Now who was shouting? Tom was being as quiet as a church mouse on tiptoe. Which isn't easy in wellies.

In the hall, Grandma was clinking like a milkmaid.

"What are you doing, Gran?" he asked

"Unlocking windows, duckie," she replied, rattling keys in her lumpy hands.

"I'll help," he said, taking the keys. "Hold up a minute though, Gran. We should leave the house locked while we're at church."

Grandma sighed. "Unlocking windows sets the soul free on its journey to Heaven," she said. "But I'm keeping the front bay shut. I'll not have him floating about near Nellie Pyefinch. I want his soul going out our back passage, Tom."

Tom couldn't understand much, because her teeth were still in the Toby jug on the landing.

"Mam's shouting for you," he told her, his face stern, "and she looks like a sheep bearing down."

"Oh, Tom, it'll be the babe coming. Quick, love. Give us the keys. Unlocking doors helps the bairn's arrival into the world."

To speed things up, Tom helped her, but it was against his best judgement. He took her arm to steer her to the kitchen, turning his head away from the front room.

"Careful, Mary," Grandma said to Mam in the kitchen, "you know what they say. Drop a knife on the floor and the next visitor will be a man. And I'd say the midwife would be a more blessed choice, duck."

"Jesus wept, our Mother, I'll bless anyone who can get me upstairs, bring this little one into the world and mash that salmon."

Tom guided Lily's hand away from the tin-opener. Mam sat down with a heavy sigh. And shot up again.

"Oh, there's no time," she cried. "How can this happen today of all days? And with Len up to his armpits in lambs."

Tom thought about this. Farming couldn't stop for funerals, or for babies. Women spent too much time talking, if you asked him. It was easy, really. Mam should go upstairs with Grandma, while he ran to the barn for Dad. Lily could sit with the lamb. She'd stay put if Tom gave her a crust.

But both women needed help up the stairs first.

"Tom, please be a very big boy and run to the shop," his mother said, her voice crackling with pain. "Ask if you can use the telephone. Here's the number and some money. Say to come quick."

Tom patted her leg, biting his lip. He had helped with the lambing. And he could stir gravy without it catching. He'd even driven a tractor in the top field. Sort of. He'd sat on Granddad's knee with his big warm hands guiding Tom's on the steering-wheel. But Tom had never used a telephone before.

Mam paused on the top stair. "Mother," she asked Gran, "why have you brought up the cake-knife?"

Grandma eased herself up to the landing, Tom pushing hard from behind. "I'll pop it under your bed, love," she panted. "Cuts the pain in two."

Tom left the women to their mysterious ways, blethering about boiling the kettle. Lord knew why. Maybe Granddad was going to wake up soon for his cup of tea.

Tom pulled a thick crust off the loaf for Lily, buttering it to the edges the way she liked it. He wasn't allowed to use knives, but after a rummage in the drawer for a substitute, he found the old ivory shoe-horn and that did the job just as well. Lily sat on the floor by the range and laid the slice down between bites as an offering to her doll, who remained dispassionate despite the growls of, "Get that down your neck. You've got a busy day." It was a good job Tom hovered for a bit, jangling the important coins in his pocket, because he was in the right spot to divert the bread from a soaking when the lamb tiddled on the floor.

His heart was scooting about like a sheepdog, herding his thoughts. Telephone call, tell Dad. Now, what else did he have to remember? Oh, yes. Visitors were coming to see Granddad before the funeral and then back again for the Battenberg. That's why the lid was off the box. People had to pay their, what was it... oh, *brassy pecks*, or something. Some sort of money, he supposed. Maybe they gave the coffin-driver a threepenny bit to drive Granddad home from the churchyard. The baby would be here by then and the celebration would be as huge as harvest.

Tom scurried past the front room, but rushed back to check Lily still sat at her station. Yes, she was singing lullabies, although now her doll lay on the old mauve towel on the floor. And in the crate, the lamb was draped with petticoat and bloomers.

Tom hurried back out on his mission and full tilt into the first early mourner on the door-step.

Mam was trusting him to hurry, so he refused to be side-tracked by beautiful Auntie Dolly wrapped in her furs and cradling a paper bag of jelly babies.

Grandma and Mam always said Auntie Dolly had never done a day's work in her life. Tom thought it would be hard for her with all those jingly bracelets and tiny skirts like cake frills. Not to mention the heels. They were like a pair of stilts sinking into the mud.

He invited her inside in his politest man-of-the-house fashion.

"In you come. Heels off, please. Mam said the lino's suffered enough. I've got to go!" he yelled, sweeping past, almost toppling her into the chicken-coop. "Lily's by the range with an orphan," he shouted over his shoulder. "Don't let her near the trifle!"

Tom would have loved Auntie to swoop as usual and gather him into her soft, lilac jersey.

But today he was a man-on-a-mission. Men didn't get cuddled and fed sweets. Tom wouldn't be tempted. Not even for the reddest jelly baby.

He shouted into the barn entrance. "Dad! Auntie's here. Mam's gone off to bed. Grandma's upstairs with a knife and Lily's by the fire. Auntie's watching the trifle."

There. That should put Dad in the picture.

Tom ran on. This was an even bigger mission than Granddad's Day Out up his back passage or whatever it was. After all, Granddad could do it all from his box. Tom was having to run like the clappers.

He stopped at the shop door and peered through the window. It was packed inside. He'd never be seen among all those people and shopping-baskets. He squeezed in and stood on the mat by the pig-man's wife. She reminded him of a good ham, plump and pink-cheeked, her hair reddish like the breadcrumb coat.

"Ooh look, if it isn't Tom from Valley Farm," she said to the entire shop.

"It *is* me, actually," he replied.

They all stopped talking and turned to look. Their staring smiles seemed to burn into his face. After a long silence, they started talking to each other about it being "a cruel day for the lad, that's-for-certain-sure", and, in more of a whisper, "hardly fair and fitting how the devil handed the old sod such a ruddy long innings, eh?"

The coins for the call sweated in Tom's hand. The questions stewed in his head like old tea in the pot. He was quivering inside his gabardine mac. His wellies were rubbing his legs because he had his short trousers on today and his eyes felt like boiled gooseberries. Furious with himself, he tried not to blink. With all the rushing about he'd forgotten that this was a sad day for the village. Everyone in the shop was wearing black for Granddad's Passing On and were bringing flans or buns or parsnip wine for the wake.

They said good things about Granddad. They said he knew the land like the back of his hand and could find his way home from the Five Bells blindfold. He knew more about farming than any man and more about Nellie Pyefinch than he should. And he was a lucky old bugger because he was so loved.

Tom's tears ran unchecked.

Tweed coats engulfed him. A lace-edged hanky and a humbug were pressed into his palm, the one without the coins. Someone asked what he needed in the shop. Was it toffees or was it a bit of luncheon-meat for his Mam's baps? Someone said it would be chutney, because they didn't make their own at Valley Farm. Tom knew that because Mam had once thrown the preserving-pan at the kitchen wall.

"Can I call the nurse?" he said with a sniff.

Their smiles made him feel a bit sick. He'd never seen that many teeth up close.

"Don't you mean the undertaker?" they chanted. "Bit late for the nurse now, duckie."

"Your Granddaddy's not in hospital any more, pet," the pig-man's wife said, her jowls wobbling by his face.

"But we need her for Mam," Tom said, his lips quivering in the same way as her cheeks. He wanted to tell them the baby was coming today. Quite sensible of it really, to arrive in time to see Granddad when he woke up.

But no one listened to what a child said. They were too busy deciding what he meant.

"Muddled up, isn't he?" they muttered.

"Bless him," they whispered.

The door flew open, along with a dozen mouths. Dolly burst in, furs flying, Lily in her arms and soil-caked stilettos stuffed in her pockets.

"It's coming!" she shrieked.

The babble began again. They said Dolly was making no more sense than Tom.

"Who'll hold my hand at the funeral if Mam's still waiting for the nurse to bring the baby?" he said. But no one heard.

His dad was going to be one of the four men lifting up the coffin. *Shawl-wearers*, Tom thought they were called. Or something like that. But Tom couldn't imagine him in anything patterned or lacy. Dad smelt of pig shite and wore the biggest boots in the valley.

Auntie Dolly was to stop at the house to get the tea mashing. Ma had said she wasn't having her taking her coat off in church. "She's bound to wear that frock that looks like a pair of puppies are fighting for space and about to jump clear of the neckline," she said.

Tom wasn't sure about that. Auntie Dolly wasn't a doggy sort. She had a bald canary with beak-rot, but he didn't think she'd put him up her jumper.

Grandma would probably stay close to Granddad. She never left his side after he fell ill. When he was getting too thin, Tom had heard her whispering, "Have my last potato, Vic. Here you are, duckie. Try to eat it up."

Today, she might tell him to hurry home before the Battenberg's all gone. Once Tom had remembered how she stewed and fretted when Granddad was struggling to get his food down, he had to scrub at his face with the hanky before Lily saw. He tried not to get the lace bit too drenched.

Lily deposited a well-chewed jelly-baby onto Auntie Dolly's furry bosoms and reached her plump arms out to Tom.

That brought him to his senses. He'd be holding Lily's hand! No one would need to hold his.

Auntie was like a flamingo in a pond of moor-hens, wading delicately through them all to the telephone. All Tom had to do was run back home.

In control once more, he strode off carrying Lily, her legs wrapped round him and her wellies bashing against his legs.

Swallowing the last tear, he stopped to think about things, and to shift Lily to his other arm. When Grandma and Mam cried about Granddad, they said they were grieving. And today it was his turn for it.

He still didn't know how to make a telephone call, but he knew about crying for someone you loved and feeling better after. It was all right. It was worth the snot clogging up your hanky.

He didn't even mind so much about the coffin. Odd about the open lid, though. People were always on at him to *close* things. Doors, for instance. And books when it was bed-time. And jam jars with maggots in. Odd people, grown-ups.

Tom and Lily arrived home and warmed up in the kitchen, the sight of the spread making them ravenous. With just the clock-ticking silence and the lamb sleeping in peace, they were in the best place, Tom reckoned. It was here at this table that he and Granddad sorted their fishing tackle.

It must be time to tidy himself up for the funeral, so he drummed the heels of his wellies against the table-leg to whack the mud off. He straightened Lily's frock and tried to comb her hair. Her squealing was drowned out by the nurse's car juddering into the yard like gun fire. Yells came from upstairs. The silence was over.

He could hear Dad's footsteps making the floorboards bounce in the room above and the nurse rushing through the door and up the stairs.

The tall coffin-driver from the black car put his head round the door and gave Tom a salute.

"In charge of the wake, are you, young sir?"

Lily looked up at him. "What's that?" she asked.

She was always saying that now. It drove Tom mad sometimes because people always answered her.

"Well, the wake's for the family and friends of the person what's passed on," the man explained, removing his hat and crouching to Lily's level. "You'll think about 'im. Talk about 'im. 'ave a sherry or two. Or a glass of milk in your case. Like a party, but without no guest of honour."

"Granddad not coming?" Lily asked, pouting.

"No, love. He'll not be able to make it. Party's over for the old soak...er... party's over for the old gentleman, love. But, tell you what, someone else'll be the VIP. Just listen to that!"

High-pitched wails tore through the house. Dad's feet were running above them, across the landing to his wife and new child.

VIP? Vanilla Ice-cream Pudding? Violet the Inormous Pig? They did have a bent-eared Gloucester Old Spot sow with that name, but Dad said she were elevenpence-halfpenny short of a shilling. Tom decided it meant Vic Is Passing. That was the only thing that sounded true.

"Tom!" Grandma called from the landing, "The keys worked! They've brought your baby brother into the world. And your Granddad's up there now, happy as Larry."

Tom got to his feet, his mind far fuller than his stomach, and headed for the hall with Lily in tow.

No wonder the house felt cold. Grandma had opened every window. Jesus wept, the things grown-ups got away with. And who on earth was Larry when he was at home?

He thought about all that had happened today. With each window he shut, he felt the truth clicking into place. Granddad wasn't coming back afterwards. Not even for the cake. They were having the party without him.

'Wake' was one of those surprise-words. Out-of-the-blue it had a second meaning that only grown-ups knew about. Grown-ups sent you on wild-goose chases with words.

Oh well, he'd worked it all out by himself in the end, this whole death business. 'Wake' had bog-all to do with eyes opening. Grandma's keys and knives made more sense. And that was saying something. Maybe it was best just to feel things instead of saying them. Trust your *ink-stinks*, as Dad always said.

Tom reached out a hand to Lily. "I'll take you to meet our new brother," he said.

"Bye, Miss Pyefinch," Lily whispered to her doll. "Grieve by yourself now, please. The Lamb of God is looking down on you."

Miss Pyefinch, tucked into the sleeping orphan's woolly flank, had a blue tear crayoned on her cheek.

The new baby's screwed-up face, wrinkled brow and toothless mouth looked beautiful to Tom. And familiar too. Maybe Granddad had come back to them after all.

Tom seized the knife from under the bed a second before Lily made a grab for it. Grandma took it from him. "Well, that did the trick all right. Half the pain, eh, Mary? And I was right about our first visitor being a man."

"The babe, Mother?" asked Mam. "Hardly a man yet!"

"No, Mary," Grandma said. "Not the babe. I mean our Tom." She passed him the warm bundle.

Mam was smiling and crying at the same time. And Dad's face was flushed and his eyes flooded with blue, same as they always were after a session at the Five Bells with Granddad.

But Tom understood now. He might still be wondering why the nurse didn't have a better car for bringing babies, but he'd learnt one or two important things. When people Pass On, it really is a long hike somewhere without popping back for your tea. Not even to fetch your spare teeth. So folk are dead right to be sad.

Plus, he'd learnt that grown-ups speak a right load of hogwash. Also, Battenberg's still heavenly, even when a wet lamb's been lying on it.

And, as he clutched the sweet warmth that was his new baby brother, the biggest surprise of all was that tears, like words, can have more than one meaning.

A Safe House for Elephant Ten

Marnie's nose was running. Her chin was wet. She was hunched on the sofa, knees drawn up to her chin in contemplation.

Ella watched her daughter with mounting concern. The nature programme was stirring her, like a spoon reaching deep into the sediment of her mind.

A dry plain stretches for miles. A family of elephants twist the huddles of trees into forlorn shapes, the only outlines on the god-forsaken horizon. The earth is parched bronze and the air still. Dry, forgotten leaves rustle. They make the only sound.

Ella looked at the tired canvas chair and the corduroy sofa, which sported a patch covered with shiny parcel-tape where other sad children's shoe-buckles had worn it away. She had expected to loathe the furniture, a job lot from a clearance sale for the desperate. She was used to better things. But when you have nothing to wear or sit on, even something worn-out becomes a gift.

The herd moves on. Ponderous and patient, they search for the disappearing forests, desperate to reclaim their land.

Ella sat by Marnie and watched her slippers slide off. Her feet were black-soled from the trampled carpet. Too many shoes, over too many years. Ella had gone into the charity shop and bought a carpet sweeper that moaned at the layered decades of dirt without collecting a crumb.

The herd shambles through powdery white river beds, their ashen skin gathering into elderly folds.

Ella picked up the slippers and pushed them onto Marnie's feet. She smoothed Marnie's tangled hair back from her ashen cheeks, caught the flood from her nose with a tissue.

The side of Ella's face was sore and her tongue probed the gap in her mouth where two teeth were missing. Three of her fingertips were gone, mangled to a figgy-looking paste and infected by the time she sought help. The nurses had severed and dressed them, frowning at her accident. Tried to keep her safe.

A stampede casts a veil of dust, obscuring the picture. Reason and logic form no part of the charge. Elephants turn into an earthly thunderstorm. Villages crumble in their harrowing path. Thirst drives the herd on.

Ella had never rebelled. Her future was a happy, straight line of blue-crayon horizon.

At Marnie's age, she watched her own mother roll pastry, blanket fruit inside it, pinch its edges with her light fingers. Sugar crystals sparkled on the cooked crust. Every pie a familiar creation. Ella wanted to leave school without fanfare, swathe herself in aprons and oven warmth. She wanted to sculpt pies and blow the heat from the scalding fruit to protect her child's mouth.

The elephants bellow. Their habitat has shrunk. Men have torn down the trees anchoring their soil. The earth is too disturbed to function. They blunder into flooded plains.

Up in the tenth floor flat, once the heavy door had creaked shut at last, its lumbering metal arm straining as if to extend Ella's fear of following footsteps, the air smelt of peace. The echoing corridors and concrete stairs vanished. Ella switched the fire on, Marnie jumped on the sofa and they smiled at each other in the glow of the bar-heater. Ella could bake pies here.

The elephants veer from the path. Instinct leads them to a life-saving tangent. Hundreds of rounded footsteps leave scant imprints on the scurrying, shifting soil. Small pockets of trees are ripped at the roots and discarded. The hunt for their huge old plains goes on.

Up in their flat, Ella and Marnie spent most days watching their television screen. Jubilant rain splashed, skittish on the windows. They listened to it and ate jam sandwiches. It was heaven.

The elephant mother drinks deeply from a shallow pool in the centre of a scrubby copse. Her baby copies joyfully.

Marnie had a beaker of yellowish tap water and Ella pretended the budget coffee was nectar. It was easy. She had been safe for days. No knock, no squeak of large trainers in the corridor.

The herd stiffens. Shots pierce the silence. The baby is dead. A cloud of desert dust hides the scene.

Ella watched Marnie grow restless and tearful, her nose pouring. She asked questions, but Marnie still didn't talk much, not even now they were safe. Safe from the shouts, the fists, the fear.

The herd is crowded into a reserve. There is no resistance. Their world has changed too much.

It wasn't safe to go out, in case he was watching, but it would be glorious in the flat when the rain finally stopped. Shafts of sunshine would flash through the safety bars on the window and make stripes across the sofa.

But Ella would never be sure if it was safe to stay in. If an axe might split through the door.

The programme finished with a replay of the tiny elephant falling to the ground in slow motion. Marnie's eyes stared, unblinking, as the credits rolled.

Ella saw Marnie look across to the glass elephants on top of the television-set, the only ornament she took when they fled. The big one led nine others of decreasing size. Trunks were coiled around the tail of the elephant in front.

Elephant Ten was missing. The baby was gone. And Marnie was finding it hard to breathe.

Ella encouraged the child to blow her nose and discovered that Marnie was trying to make tiny Elephant Ten a home there, safe from the hunters, just before the footsteps in the corridor reached the door.

THE RELIABLE SITTER

"Ah, Diana, do come in," June said to the babysitter on the step. "Don't worry, we'll have him settled soon."

Diana glanced back at the Sunday evening avenue. The September wind was sending clouds in batches across the late sun and stripping the trees. Their branches were playing tricks with the light. Inside, she could hear the wailing upstairs was of the intense variety.

Diana stepped onto the plastic matting in the hall. Her shoes made it crackle.

"Just pop your shoes in the rack, Diana. Don't forget, will you!" June said. She laughed with her usual nervous yelp.

Diana never forgot. She placed them between June's Saturday suede loafers and Harry's office brogues. They looked dainty there. Size four compared with June's eight and Harry's eleven.

June beckoned Diana into the lounge, where the television murmured.

"No louder than volume three, please," she said. "Otherwise Bobby will be disturbed."

Diana considered that Bobby sounded pretty disturbed already. His lament penetrated the lounge ceiling, drowning the voices of the screen medical team. June and Harry had the colour set too high. Diana watched a dazzling white ambulance tear away from the hospital. The camera swept to the blood-orange face of the driver.

"Come through to the kitchen, Diana."

A jug of squash waited on a tray with a tumbler and a plate of plain biscuits.

"Remember to eat and drink in here, won't you? Promise me now!"

Diana gave June her Girl Guide salute and was rewarded with the fearful smile June adopted when she thought the sitter might be mocking her.

They returned to the lounge and Diana was invited to sit in the chair closest to the television set and given a magazine listing her choice for that evening. The ceiling groaned from Harry's pacing.

"Teething," June explained.

Diana imagined huge Harry, a man who appeared to be moulded out of a block of pork sausage-meat, blubbering and gnawing at a rusk. She giggled.

June frowned and went to stand by the empty grate. She repositioned a pale, plastic carnation in the vase on the mantelpiece.

"Now Diana, as usual, the rules. No telephone calls. No slamming doors. Please raise the toilet seat before you flush. Water spots fly up onto the underside otherwise and pepper it with stains. No feet up on the armchair. And absolutely no boyfriends!"

Diana nodded. The crying stopped with a finality that made June laugh again.

"Little monkey! Worn himself out, I expect. Just dropped off in Harry's arms. Harry will come down as soon as he finishes tucking him in. Then I'll pop up and check him myself before we go."

Diana watched June straightening the magazines on the coffee table. Totally sexless, Diana decided. Beige jumper, peach skirt and neutral tights. Her breasts swung like hammocks full of wet sponges, living separately from their owner. She seemed unaware of them, as if they were neighbours out at work all day and never spoken to.

Her hair was shorn like a schoolboy on his first day, revealing a long, but graceless neck. She plodded to the hall to put her size eights on the matting, ready for the night out at Quality Inn.

Diana imagined June and Harry at the salad trough, their spoons chasing slimy bits of avocado and cucumber.

"Mmmm," they would say at intervals while they chewed, listening to disjointed segments of the conversations around them.

"Lovely and tender," they would say twice each, steak bouncing away from their knives.

June would acquire a film of oil on her upper lip. Harry's porous yellow teeth would blacken from the rough red wine.

Diana sat still for half an hour after they left, then turned off the television to listen for the tap on the door.

A caravanning magazine gleamed at her from the pile. She shuddered. It reminded her of her parents bundled in deck-chairs on holiday, slopping tea into their plastic beakers from the tartan Thermos, watching youthful families kick balls and charge with desperate toddlers to the soaking wet toilets.

While she waited, the crying began, soft at first, then gradually louder. She had expected it. The half-hour of peace was usually followed by the first small wail.

She never tensed. That's why June and Harry trusted her to do a good job. Diana was calm and measured in her approach. She liked to exaggerate that aspect of her character, because she knew it reassured June and Harry. It gave them faith in her.

She opened the windows. The wind roared in. The neighbours were packing away garden tools while their raked leaves were beginning to fly out of their neat mounds. The man on the left and the woman on the right glanced up at the sudden noise of Bobby's crying.

The tap on the door came on the dot. Russell never interfered with the arrangements. Diana had told him she would not let him in if he were late.

The crying would peter out soon. Tonight, Bobby's pattern seemed to be Type Two. Type One was fussy and fairly constant until late in the evening. Very annoying with its predictable staccato, but could be ignored if she kept the door closed. Type Two had the loud start, reaching a crescendo by about eight-thirty, softening by degrees.

"Straight upstairs?" Russell gasped.

Diana wished he wouldn't. She was never sure whether he panted so hard from jogging here or from genuine desire. At least he was on time and ready to start, though.

"Of course," she said. "We may not have as long this time."

"Better get down to it then."

"Yes. They booked, which means they won't be hanging about for a table. I suppose it depends on whether they have the starter. But we've at least an hour."

"Let's go then."

Diana slid out of her clothes as soon as they entered June and Harry's bedroom. The crying became harsher. Russell hesitated.

"Don't know if I can concentrate with that noise, Diana."

"He always quietens after this breathless sort of crying. Can you hear that gasp he makes every minute or so? That's a sign he's almost ready to stop."

"But shouldn't you go in there?"

"Oh, Russell, we have this every time. He'll be fine. He always is. Trust me."

Russell struggled out of his jeans and shivered, lily-white in the darkening room.

"Bloody cold. Can't we shut the window?"

"No. June wants them open. Fresh air and all that. Now come on."

Russell skipped the tender kisses. Diana had decided they wasted time. He lay on the bed and let her climb on top of him.

But at the supreme moment, the crying rose to its highest

pitch, a scream Diana had never heard before. Shrill and persistent. She paused.

"You should go in there," Russell mumbled from beneath her, flagging.

"No. It'll pass," she said, her body resuming its well-calibrated rhythm to resurrect him. Russell quivered. His euphoric moans almost drowned the baby out.

But just as their moment returned, a distraught howl made them freeze. It was the most haunting sound Diana had ever heard.

"Fox?" Russell gasped, clinging to hope.

"No. It's him again."

"Better go then."

"I'll be quick."

Diana returned within seconds. Bobby had quietened down as soon as she reached the room.

"How did you do that?"

"Easy. I'm an expert."

"But what the hell was wrong? He sounded like he was really ill or something."

"Just being a nuisance as usual. Type Three."

"Three?"

"There are different types of crying. I know the first two, but now there seems to be a third as well."

She tried to resume their position once more, but Russell had retreated and there was no time left to encourage him back to where they were.

"I can't now, Di. Too many interruptions. I have to concentrate on it, you know."

"Well so do I. But I'm here to babysit, remember. I can't manage to do everything at once. And you're harder work than bloody Bobby sometimes. Takes me forty minutes to sort you out. Forty seconds for him."

Russell slid off the bed and pulled his socks on. His back shone white in the new moonlight that sliced through the undrawn curtains. The floral fabric flapped in the wind, blistering his skin with goose-pimples.

"It's bloody freezing, Di."

"All right. I can shut it now."

Bobby was quiet, but Russell remained tense about the earlier crying. Diana agreed to check again. The evening had been a letdown. She was unprepared for straying off plan like this. It felt like failure.

"You don't seem to care," Russell said, head in his hands.

"I do, Russ. Let's give it another quick go."

"For God's sake, I don't mean that. I mean *him*. That poor kid. You're hard, you are."

"I'm not hard. I'm not," she called to Russell as he left the room.

Russell didn't bother to answer, tucking his shirt into his jeans as he hurried downstairs.

"Russ, I'm back here next Friday at seven," she called from the landing. "They're going bowling."

Russell picked his size sevens off the rack, his socks slithering on the plastic matting. "Don't think I can make it, Di, actually."

She held her breath as she ran down. The end was coming.

"It's been fun, Di," he said, stepping back as she reached him, "but you should probably focus on the kid a bit more. Anyway, it's only a matter of time before we get caught. Let's cut our losses before the truth gets out."

He kissed her cheek, his chapped lips like an old leaf.

Diana wanted to cry, but she had things to do. The bed covers would need straightening, all the windows closing, and Russell had used the toilet. As she erased the water spots, she thought about the emptiness of next Friday.

She couldn't stay at home, making sandwiches for her parents, watching the cress stick out from the edges of their mouths. She wanted an evening free from their devotion to their one child, who had arrived as their skin was already beginning to desiccate. And she needed one evening free from her devotion to them.

Fridays were for pulling away from the benign power that gripped them to one another like iron filings to a magnet.

She dashed to the hall and telephoned Rob Moran. He was always quizzing her about the babysitting. She guessed Russell had bragged at school. She suggested Friday to Rob. Seven-thirty on the dot, she told him. He mustn't let her down. She was reliable and expected her visitors to be the same.

She waited in the armchair for June and Harry to come home. In the peace of late evening on Sycamore Avenue, all the cars idle and all the curtains closed against the approaching night, she glanced around and noticed a new photograph on the sideboard. It had been taken at a portrait studio and framed in silver.

June and Harry were dressed in their enormous matching white shirts, beaming against a pure white background. So much white that their faces seemed detached and huge. Their blue eyes shone with infantile hope. Diana turned away, unusually close to tears.

For the first time she felt their misery. Some sort of internal blade twisted. She felt compelled to leave the bedspread wrinkled and rucked. Let it betray her. Give birth to her secret. Then they could shout at her. She could feel bad and beg for forgiveness.

She slipped upstairs just as their car turned into the avenue. She went into the nursery with its pristine empty cot and immaculate row of stuffed toys. It was time to close this window. June and Harry liked to keep them open until the end of the evening, so the neighbours in their gardens could believe in Bobby.

Diana shut the window. She rewound and ejected the new and startling Type Three recording from the tape machine.

June and Harry must have visited friends with a baby again, taking with them the reel-to-reel and microphone. June hadn't mentioned this latest recording. Perhaps she wanted to ensure Diana didn't become complacent. Put the sitter through her paces.

They made copies of the recordings for their friends. Diana imagined the besotted new parents finding it enchanting, this permanent record of how Baby sounded at birth, at three months, at six months. They pinned a downy lock of hair from the first haircut to the suede innards of a small box and preserved the first pair of tiny shoes in a coat of silver plating. Now they owned the voice too. It gave June and Harry such a boost to provide this service for their grateful friends, who had no idea what a service it provided for June and Harry too.

Diana had felt wrong-footed by that piercing cry. But at least she felt prepared for next time now she'd heard it all the way through. Best to know what you were dealing with.

She cradled the reel of tape in her hand. Silent and solid, it soothed her, dulling the edge of her pain. She flipped it over and over in her palm. June and Harry would never find another babysitter as loyal as Diana.

She smiled, fully recovered. Her heartbeat slowed to normal. She made the bed, dashing around it, aware of the time, taking care to tease the coverlet into place and twitch the pillows into shape.

She took a step back to admire her work. You couldn't tell. Some secrets should never be told.

The car wheels were scattering the loose stones on the gravel drive. She ran down, straightening her blouse, and clicked on the television-set to the lurid, bleeding tie and neon-pink face of the newscaster. She put on a sparkling smile of her own, ready to greet them and ask politely how their evening had gone.

THE INVITATION

Ruby were right excited that she were coming home with me. Mostly she kept herself all calm, floated along like a coot on a pond, but today she clapped her thin hands and jumped on the spot. I was smiling, but there were a squirming inside me. Like on Big Dipper. Like those mornings when you wake up and know something's happening, but not if it's good or bad. Like a bit of birthday and a bit of dentist rolled up together.

She asked me questions all day. It were right good. I told her about my bedroom with the yellow cupboard built-in and my puppies on the wall. She asked if we had a real puppy. Mine were just dog-food labels though. She kept asking if we had things we didn't have. I had to keep disappointing her.

"Have you got tropical fish?"

"I won a goldfish at the fair. Fetched him home in a plastic bag."

"We have seven angelfish."

"Oh."

"What's your goldfish called?"

"He were dead by the time I got home."

"Oh."

Her school dress was the proper one for summer. Her Mam made it from the special green daisy material at Bradshaw's. It had that zigzag stuff round the armpits and a little silver charm hanging off the zipper. It were a different charm every day. I liked the curly snail and Ruby's favourite was the pony with his front legs up. My wrong dress were Alice Bagstaff's and before that it were Sharon Clitheroe's and before that it were Sharon's Mam's. It came from the Home Stores when it still had gas lights and it's flitting from house to house all the way down our terrace. It'll be Annie Wainwright's next, but it might have to stop there. It's that worn out no one knows what colour it's meant to be.

The sun were boiling our heads on the long walk home. The others stared and shouted, "How come *she's* going to yours then?" The worst thing was, "Did your Mam say she could?"

Ruby kept watching me with that hard face she had sometimes, making me say, "Yeah, course it's all right." I had to screw my eyes up against the sun to look at her. Her hair shone like the polished black tiles in my auntie's privy. I glared at the others and pulled up my sock.

The ice-cream money were sweating in my shoe. I'd saved it for weeks for this day, the coins in a strip of tissue wound round and round them. It burned up a right bad blister. I'd taken the tissue out and unravelled it a few times to look at the pennies. One were right black and I were worried that Mr Beavis would shake his head at it. I stroked my thumb over the bumps of Her Majesty's head so many times it were in danger of being rubbed out. Then Beavis would really have summat to shake his fat head about. But it's not that easy to wipe heads off. The great lady were safe with me.

Beavis had put the prices up, so I bought Ruby her Witch's Hat she kept going on about and was left with a ha'penny that wouldn't buy owt. I reckoned on getting a lick, but she was a bit tight-lipped again.

"Why can't I have a Ninety-Nine?" She asked that ninety-nine times.

"'Cause the Flakes are another bloody penny, Ruby."

Mr Beavis reached across his cones and tried to clip me round the ear. Couldn't get me, though. He might tell me dad at the Lamb and Flag. I'll pray he forgets. Mam and Dad listen to me pray every night, but they don't get to hear my secrets. I add them on in the two minutes for silent confessing.

Like, "Please can I have a nicer Mam and Dad?" Or "Wouldn't split your face in half to smile down on me from Heaven now and then, would it? Have you forgot I'm here?"

I talk to Jesus, not God. God is a scary old git in a white dress, but Jesus is quite a lot nicer. He fetched up with a bad crowd through no fault of his own and I felt sorry for him screwed onto the cross at the end.

Ruby was still moaning at Rochester Drive and sulking by Cemetery Row.

"Fancy you not knowing what a Witch's Hat is."

"I bloody do! It's a cornet with a lolly stuck head-first in the ice-cream. Everyone knows that."

"But it should have the Flake. *Our* ice-cream man always sticks one in. Sometimes two. My father once had three, actually."

I felt sick. I bet her mam's sink didn't have ruddy great big dents out of it. I didn't want Dad eating slices of *Mother's Pride* rolled up from the packet on the table. And Ruby would stare at the hairs bushing out of the holes in his vest. I hoped and prayed we had a bit of toilet paper left. Couldn't have her wiping her bum on the *Express*, could we?

She dropped the ice-lolly. A rare purple one it were. Beavis usually had yellow or green. She squealed and stood there like a right lemon. I picked it up, but she wouldn't touch it.

"Lick it for me," she said.

"You what?"

"Lick the gravel off. *I* can't. And I don't want to waste your money."

Her face were crumpling. Like my sock this morning. Had a slapped leg for gabbing in assembly. It weren't bad, but the teacher yanked the sock down and it wouldn't pull up again. He'd snapped me garter. The others pointed at the red finger marks all day. He did the same to Eunice, but she had her sister Stella to wait for her and link arms. I saw Ruby watching all the slaps, but she ran off after.

It were still a good day because I had Ruby coming home, but I had to spend it holding me sock up. And now I had to stop Ruby from going to pieces. Couldn't take a misery guts home now, could I?

I licked the lolly, then she made me wipe it with me best hanky so she wouldn't get my germs. Then I rammed the bloody thing back in her cornet. I had bits in me mouth from the pavement, so I spat them out and the others made disgusted noises from behind the pillar box. They couldn't fetch their eyes off me and my new friend and her bloody Witch's Hat. I pretended they weren't there. I melted them away with that fierce hot bit in my head that stops up tears.

Didn't stop me feeling sick, though. There were frothing in my belly and my throat filled with sour stuff. That started as we turned the corner into our road. I'd have traded my *Bunty* annual for another taste of blackcurrant ice. Even if it turned bitter after one second, I would have still liked it, I was that dry. Tongue too big for my mouth.

I could see our gate. I could see our Mam with pegs in her mouth. She had that short dress on so you could see the knotted blue strings in her legs. Her head was all hedgehoggy with curlers. I had prayed to that blasted Jesus for this not to happen. I had prayed for the cornflower skirt and a smile. But they were just for picnics. I could see the frown carved into the space between her eyebrows from as far back as the Tanners' gate.

"Let's walk really slow, Ruby."

"Why? I want to get out of the sun now. And I need to wash my hands. They're sticky from that stupid ice-cream. And I want to be in time to watch *Blue Peter*."

We didn't have telly. I couldn't say. I told her about cutting out pictures from Mam's old magazine and sticking them in a scrapbook. I knew there weren't many good pictures left. Only adverts for varicose veins and women's moustaches. But I said she could have her own page. And I told her about *Ludo* and how I was allowed to get that out on the dinner table if Dad didn't have his racing-pages spread out. I even told her about the game with Belinda, my doll with no head. It were a hospital game and you could choose to be the nurse, the doctor or Belinda's upset mam. Ruby looked quite interested then. I was winning again.

She pulled a face when I said it might be pilchard salad for tea. I reckon she wouldn't know a pilchard if one fetched up and played hopscotch with us. She cheered up when I said we'd have iced buns after, but that was a lie. Just to soften up her gob like.

"Do you have a paddling-pool?" she asked. "Ours is red. It was the biggest in the shop."

"Hose might be mended."

We reached the gate.

I didn't breathe while we waited, me and Ruby together. Mam was crouched by the laundry basket with her knees splayed out, dark stains under her arms. The sick feeling was like a big fist in a boxing glove jabbing at me insides. Faster and faster it banged, as Mam started to heave herself up, her smoke yellowing the white sheets. Her cigarette quivered on her bottom lip, even when her mouth dropped open.

She wouldn't let us in. She stood blocking our gate. I couldn't look at Ruby. I had to fix my eyes on a little tuft of brown grass trying to grow by the gate-post where next-door's cat piddles. At least the tears didn't come, thank Jesus.

I tried my small polite voice. "Can Ruby play, please?"

I don't think Mam heard me, she were that vexed. Just kept pointing. I'm not sure where. Just in the direction of the other end of town where all the flats are. And the new parades of shops with the silky stuff and the spicy smells. And the restaurants called Curry Houses.

Me dad always said, "Bloody spices. It's not natural, it's not."

Me mam would say, "Ugh!" and shudder. Told me to hold me breath if I walked past one of them sort. But not make it obvious like. Said summat about letting too many in and Eeknock Power being right about them Rivers of Blood.

I did think they'd like Ruby though. I've seen pictures of coffee in cups. Pale milky brown. And her skin were that lovely colour. And she said 'scones' properly as well.

Mam told me to get in now, or else. I watched Ruby walk away. She went backwards for the first few steps. She shrugged a tiny bit and then turned, as if it didn't matter. She can be right hard.

I'd started praying for her to be my friend after she told me she were having a party. I might get an invitation, she said, if she could play at ours first.

I prayed hard for that. Never had one before. People don't have parties round here. Sharon had shrimp paste on crackers and tinned pear flan when she turned seven and I was told to come for that and a game of blind man's bluff. Her dad cheated with his blindfold and grabbed our legs. That weren't a party.

Ruby was having a real party, with things in pastry and purses with sequins all over to give as prizes. I prayed for one of them. I even asked that blithering idiot, God, as well as Jesus. Ruby's mother were going to stick balloons on the front door.

Anyway, I watched Ruby go and Mam growled at me to get in. She squeezed my arm so tight it were like a Chinese burn. I didn't have sleeves on account of it being summer, so it were extra hard. She didn't speak a word, just looked right mad. I didn't cry all the way upstairs, all the way across the landing and into me room.

Only when I lay on my bed. That's when these right hot tears kept on coming. I kept them silent though and I did a lot of praying.

The next day Ruby gave me the invitation and thanked me for the Witch's Hat. It were like this happened all the time. She weren't even surprised. Just set her face hard. But inside herself, I knew she was as sad as me. I felt it.

The invitation was on this little card with jig-jaggedy edges and a snip of bright red ribbon threaded along the top. The party was on Wednesday. The writing was small and neat. Her real name was Rubaida. I loved it. She had even done a proper signature. And it said *RSVP*. That could be her other name. Don't know how you blinking well say it

But it was in pencil. She said to bring it back if Mam said no. Then she'd rub my name out and try another girl. When I looked hard at my name, there were lots of little pencil-dents underneath.

I did pray extra that night, but I still weren't brave enough to ask Mam and Dad, so it didn't do owt. There were no time left. I gave her back the card. Rubbed me name out for her, I did. I unravelled the bit of ribbon though. Kept it. Tied it on Belinda's wrist. But it looked like a line of blood, as if Belinda had got herself into another nasty accident.

I walked the long way home that took me past the house on the day of the party, but there were no balloons on Rubaida's door.

ONE-HORSE TOWN

One horse don't mean nothing ever happens here. The crops are parched and the dust blows in your eyes enough to make you cry just walking. But things do happen. People disappear.

There was Jack Pole last month and now Jenny Teague. They were at my school and now they aren't. We all looked and then we looked again. We're looking again later. There's a proper search party starting out from the school.

Ain't many places to hide here. It's just a flat space with a few worn-down homes and a splintered school building in the mountain's shadow. The sun can't shine there. It has a cactus garden we tend ourselves and the granmas come and help us with trying to grow corn in a triangle at the end of the yard. That's where a stripe of light appears once a day.

My granma lives with us, her chalky eyes watching us burst the seams of the shack. I tell her about the names they call me and she listens. Never says nothing, just rocks away in her old chair, pulling at her knitting-wool with her knotty, spotty hands.

Jenny was in charge of the names and now they have to find a new leader. I know they will. Even in a one-horse town, you know there's always one who takes charge, one who pulls my good ankle from behind with a smart old yank that floors me, try as I might to hop upright on my no-good leg. One horse, one leader. That's as much as you need in one place, I reckon.

I always want to go to school, even with the names and the tripping. I come home and tell my sisters all I can remember of the teaching. If we had paper, I could write it. They yawn in my face, but I still tell them. Takes me a long time to get to school with my stick digging into the tender place under my arm where it always beds in. There's a kind of groove there. Takes longer getting home when I'm tired. We don't sleep well. Five to a mattress, with a new-born on the side, is too many. Always someone on my leg, someone in my dreams. We don't have nothing each, not one damn thing we'd call our own.

I dream of being a schoolmistress in the big town, where the ladies in long skirts whisper through the department stores, saying "Charge it to my account" and smiling gently at their easy lives. They have husbands with clean moustaches and soft hands. They have white lace kerchiefs and little children who eat soft meat and have their own rooms with their own books and their own sunlight making patterns on their own warm floor.

If you visited this massive region, if you walked right into the heart of this little inhabited bit of it nestled in the mountain's feet like a dead mouse lying at the paws of a tiger, you would put your head on one side and look at it fond-like. It's not sweet here, though. In my house, we flinch when Pa gets home.

Pa was raised by a fisty uncle with a red beard and no heart. He didn't wanna look at no one's children, a whole ton less live with one of 'em, but Pa was lumped on him, so Uncle put him to work from cock-crow to sundown and gave him a dirty hay-bed in the barn. Pa sat bolt upright every night, training a gun on the rats. He was six years old when he went there and hardly ate a decent meal until he left to make his own living at fourteen. He ain't never had a conversation with no one but the cattle and the dogs. People say he was a scavenger, but Ma says he just wanted to survive. She was the first to care. Leastways, she cooks and washes for him and keeps out of the way until he finds her, then shuts the hell up about the bruises. Too late, I guess, for him to show any caring back. He never learnt how. Guess having your brain pulped by the red uncle's fists don't help none.

Guess I won't be much use at searching. Emmy Lyons looked at my leg with a kind of sneer when the teacher said we could all help. They're going up the far side today. They reckon Jack dared hisself to climb it and froze hard some place where no one goes. Maybe he slipped into a gully, he were that skinny.

They said Jenny was that sweet on him she'd never recover. Never stopped looking. Now she's gone too. Can't say I miss her. It don't sit well with me to lie.

They all say I clubbed her to death with my stick one dark night. Woulda fallen clean over if I had.

I watch them. There's a scratchy ole wind sizzling through the grasses and I can feel how the earth just don't care. This great big dish o' dust just blows us all around not giving a damn. Just blew Jack and Jenny away.

I go inside to help with the dishes. Baby's wailing that much, it's a blessing no one ever talks none. Ma points at the cold, grey water. She frowns at the worn strip of leather round my wrist. Well, I wish she wouldn't wear that old dress with the neck kinda sagging down into lots of weary old folds. I can see her collar bones and they ain't pretty. Hard-sucked by a cur, they look.

Granma is watching out the window, as the searching figures get smaller and smaller, pulled into the shadows by the time they reach the first outcrop of boulders. Women round here do a lot of watching, waiting. Don't know what for. Ain't never getting any better in these parts.

"Ain't gonna find nothing," Granma says, screwing up her shrivelled little mouth as she turns to look at us. It makes me and Ma stop a second, that sad ole face of hers.

I loved Jack Pole. It was a secret, but Jenny guessed it. That's when the hurting and the names got ten times worse. She got him doing it too. I didn't mind. I loved it when he pushed me around, his smooth boy's skin close to me and his long boy's fingers on me. Ain't never been touched any other way than rough, anyways.

He followed me home last year and wrestled me to the dirt in the shade of the dead apple. I can still smell him. Still wear that bit of leather from some old bridle that fell out of his pocket. Went home that day with stains on my dress that earned me a ringing ear, but I never could wipe the smile off my face. Not for days and days.

Us kids don't hang around the house much after the chores. Mostly we hide out. I'm alone in the log shed tonight and the searching still goes on. No one is around, except women and old folks. And Pa, sitting with his whisky cradled in his lap. He stops seeing me clear when the bottle has an inch of that sweat-stinking stuff left.

I saw him looking at the baby in his box tonight in a kinda tender way. Head tilted a bit, eyes kinda shiny in the candlelight. Liquor had kicked in, I guess.

I sure am too cold to move. Nights are freezing here. If you dandy tourists ever think, "Hey there, what an adorable outta-the-way place, do let's spend the night," then darn well think some more. Ain't nice when the light goes.

I think about Jack and shiver. His Ma has nobody now. She's all empty-looking these days, shawl tight round her face, hollow eyes peering out, all full of pain. Jack was gonna look after her, Ma Pole says. Jenny was gonna marry him and tend the hog and chooks. Jack was gonna make the farm real good. Pretty picture. But I couldn't see it, not in a month of Sundays.

Jenny despised this one-horse town, all apart from Jack. How about a picture without you in it, Ma Pole? Just those two love-birds holdin' hands in the sunshine, Jenny's bright hair floating around her mean little face, as she takes the spot beside her man some place other than this dry old fly-strewn, god-forsook place.

Jenny could be that schoolmistress I once took a fancy being myself. When I have my daily dream, it's always Jenny's face stuck in there where mine should be. She's sharp as a tack, the teacher says. She can tell you all the names of every damn state in America and she can spell tarpaulin.

She woulda scooped up Jack Pole from his Ma's weak arms and carried him off to the big town within the year. She tramples on my dreams same goddamn way as my brothers and sisters do in the night.

I lean back on the logs and wait. The air is so cold it stings my nostrils. From inside, I can hear the cries of the baby. If I go in, I'll have to stir the boiling diapers. Diaper stew. Can't take that smell no more. The clear night air's icing up my nose again. I'm feeling kinda sick. A goat pushes against me. Damn thing stinks.

I can hear the mountain. They've found something. I throw up. The goat starts licking.

The air is whirling around me now as I stumble out of the shelter, tearful with cold. Grasses are whipping my legs. The echoes of shouts from high above chill me even more. Bad news. Those are sorrowing voices. The waiting makes me wet myself. Leastways, it warms my legs for a few seconds.

It takes forever to make out the first group under the moon, walking slow as molasses, not in that rushing way people usually move when they're frozen. These people are hunched together. Defeated. Don't wanna hurry back to us all with their news. They have a burden lit up by their lanterns. It's across the back of the horse. Jack's Ma and Jenny's folk are waiting in the schoolhouse and I swear I can hear the screams, one hot on the heels of the next.

I keep quiet. I know better than to show myself. I been keeping to myself all my life, just like my folks. We don't say our feelings. We see things that never get told. They say, "chop-that-wood-girl-feed-them-chicks-clear-that-table". But they don't say "How're ya feeling today?"

They know things, though. They just don't choose to tell folk that that baby's mine. I don't say how Granma, gun weighing down her shabby old blanket-coat, led my tormentor away to pick mountain flowers. Nor how my daddy went out at dead of night last month and came back just before sunrise with blood on his coat. One damn thing he did to show he cared.

I rub the leather chafing my wrist raw. The horse is neighin' its head off, spooked by the wind off the mountain.

QUISTON AVENUE

Quiston Avenue stretched as far as Phillip could see. The limes leaned into the wind, as if beckoning him along the pavement. Or in homage to something at the far end. He waited on the corner. The dove-grey brick of the paired houses was shimmering after the downpour, darker in patches.

Phillip had walked along other damp streets, past warm-looking shops, rain-spotted cabbages in crates and mothers talking by pillar boxes. Benches, wet and broken, compelled him to sit down, holding back the moment of arrival. The drizzle slid his fringe further over his eyes. He expected passers-by to stare, as if he were outlined in black marker pen, but they didn't. They passed by.

Before reaching the lime swathe of the avenue, he passed the parade of hairdressers wafting ammonia, restaurants selling chicken fried in orange coats and people licking grease from their thumbs.

He had never eaten takeaway, but at school they were always talking about it. He ate Bavarian ham and bitter bread and tall slices of cake speckled with caraway. But he didn't say this. He nodded when they mentioned KFC, as if he understood about meals with initials eaten from bags in bedrooms.

He didn't say about the lace cloth that draped over his knees when he sat at the table or the heavy cutlery that he helped to polish every Saturday.

Quiston Avenue roared. The wind had annexed it, tearing through the trees. They bowed away from Phillip.

Julie had told him her front door was painted yellow. He needed to walk the length of the avenue to reach it. He took out his cigarette papers and tobacco, turning to the wall for cover.

★

"Didn't know you smoked," Julie had said.

Phillip rolled, licked and lit up, knowing he would finish just as the bell rang for the end of break.

"Can you roll me one?"

He passed her his own and lit the spare from the inside pocket of his blazer. They stood in silence behind the rounders shed. Phillip listened to the football thudding against it, matching the beat of his pulse.

He felt Julie's gentle surprise. Her long auburn hair smelt of raspberries. It almost touched his sleeve when the breeze curved round the shed. He could imagine her washing it that morning in a tiled bathroom.

"You're not the type to do this," Julie said, releasing the smoke through her nose in two soft clouds. "You're so quiet I even forget you're in my class."

The sun tinted her fringe gold. Phillip could see the network of delicate green veins on her eyelids.

He ground his stub into the earth as the bell rang. He felt her hesitate, watching him.

"Phillip, do you know Quiston Avenue?"

"Yes, I know it."

The wind seethed, chasing his stub into a heap of old leaves.

"I live there," Julie said. "Want to come over?"

★

91

He couldn't see the yellow door from here, but he thought he smelt raspberries in the wind. Julie's scent was sealed inside him. Her hair swung like a silk curtain over every thought, every dream.

He knew the nap of her skirt, the row of freckles on her cheek, the way she tapped her left foot during maths tests. He knew how the sun shone on the biscuit crumbs she trailed across her desk at break. He hung around after everyone left the classroom, daring himself to lick them and feel them dissolve on his tongue.

He brushed by her whenever the chance came. She wafted pink bubble-gum, stale tobacco and the smell of her home. He had inhaled the house with the yellow door so many times now, he felt he lived there too.

He stopped. Halfway there. He had passed fifteen trees. Another fifteen bowed before him.

★

"We could have a laugh, you know," Julie had said, as they went inside from break, the echo of the bell fading.

Phillip didn't know. His grandmother didn't encourage him to laugh. In the afternoons, they boiled ham bones for soup and looked at photographs of his parents. Every day, they sat at the table at four o'clock, listening to the strong coffee drip through the filter. His grandmother would slice through the sugared crust of her plum streusel and pass the pot of whipped cream to Phillip. He spooned it out for them both. It was his task.

She wore her good dress for coffee at four, mint-blue linen, shiny from use. She swept her yellowed hair into a bun and slid on her dead daughter's bracelet, the metal warped by the crash; a piece of the past to flash in the light of the bare bulb swinging from the ceiling.

And they sat with the last few surviving pieces of thin silverware, the fine cloth and the delicate coffee cups in the bare room ten floors up, trying not to hear the tinny doors slamming around them and the brutal footfall of hope-emptied youth on the concrete stairs.

★

At the age of five, Phillip had survived the collision in Quiston Avenue. It crushed his parents. His mother's head remained attached to her neck by a sliver of sinew. Blood seeped into the drains of Quiston Avenue very quickly, owing to the downpour that had caused the dustbin lorry to swerve out of control.

Phillip came here every week and waited at this spot. Waited to feel something. Waited to cry. Waited for grief to wash over him.

The images replayed, sharp in his mind. The scream was clear, but he didn't know which of the three of them had made it. He remembered the shattered glass and twisted car. His mother's dear face, in its state of near-detachment.

Fifteen trees ahead, but he couldn't move. He saw the garden with the gnome waving, its twin house with net curtains, the broken section of kerb, the stain on the pavement that resembled India and the tar-like tyre markings on the road. He saw them all in his head every night.

And he saw them on the tablecloth. He saw them on the ceiling when he looked up at the crash of feet above. He saw them while he watched the bulb swing from its moorings, imagining the plaster cascading like shattered icing over the table.

★

Phillip wondered who would open the yellow door. A parent, a sister? Would they make him tea in a wafer-thin cup that would jitter on its saucer as he held it? Could he smoke there? Would they cut a Swiss roll into slices that would make him jammy while he sweated in the hot tea steam?

There would be questions.

"What subjects do you like at school?"

"English, Mrs Murray."

"Do you like reading?"

"Quite. But really I like English because it's a change from real life. In our council block, where the stairwells ring with scorn and despair, my grandmother pretends she is still a statesman's daughter in their high-ceilinged mansion before the war in Germany. We eat cake filled with German seeds. We speak only German. And we talk about my mangled parents. Although, to be fair, they stop being mangled when we talk about them."

But if the parents were out for the day, he would lie on Julie's bed beside her and she would say, "Phillip."

That was all he wanted. Just his name spoken aloud, her tongue unfurling the syllables the way his father used to say it in his pure Kent voice that Phillip's memory mingled with the apple tree that rained down fruit in their old garden, warm milk on bonfire night and damp lawn clippings in soft, sweet-smelling piles.

"Phillip," Julie would whisper, as she rolled off his clothes and pulled her blankets up to their chins. She would wear a soft nightdress with a ribbon-thread at the neck, like the one still hanging from a hook on the back of the bathroom door in the flat.

*

"Oh, Ted, I cannot believe we shall live here in ziss so English avenue," his mother had laughed, mispronouncing 'th' as she always did when she was excited. "It is a dream. Truly, darling."

Phillip's father had smiled at her, taking his eyes from the road halfway along Quiston Avenue.

"Oh look, the rubbish is collected on a Friday," she gabbled, her spirits soaring towards the new future.

Ted beamed and ran his fingers round the circumference of the steering wheel, tacky from rain steam and car breath.

She was in love with the new house and the quiet road and the courteous sentry of trees that brought to mind a once-glorious Berlin. She was still talking when they drove into the lorry.

Silence fell in their car after the impact. But outside, the scattered rubbish was hurled into the air. Cans, bottles and jars skated across the road. Ashes and tea leaves in newspaper parcels kept whispering and skittering over the tarmac, until the ambulance siren blasted through the stillness, drowning everything out. Phillip had always remembered the noises, insistent in his ears.

He sometimes saw a stray bit of litter caught in a hedge or drowned in a puddle on Quiston Avenue and wondered if it might be a vestige left behind from that day.

*

Another few paces and he would see Julie, but now he could only look at the collision spot. He felt compelled, however foolish it was, to lift a finger of recognition to the gnome, discreetly, in case anyone was watching behind the nets. He traced the outline of India with the toe of his shoe. He stepped into the road to the place where his mother's head had lain and watched it appear like an exotic flower, the centre streaked with red and her hair flowing all around like a sunburst of glorious petals.

He looked up at the sky, just as he always did, hoping to see a weightless bird swerve in an arc. Seconds before the crash he had seen a heron with two defeated goldfish hanging in its beak, fresh from one of Quiston Avenue's garden ponds. He watched the heron take flight just as his mother said, "I'm very happy our new door is royal blue."

She was charmed by English royalty. She believed she would

live like a princess in Quiston Avenue. The royal blue door was just before Julie's yellow one.

Phillip tried to feel the warmth of Julie's lips in his hair, her small, rounded teeth grazing his chest and her cool fingers raking at the new hairs growing there. He had imagined it often in class when he was supposed to be drawing chromosomes or squaring x.

They could have eaten burgers in cartons, a picnic spread out on the pillow.

"We'll have a laugh," she had said.

It was an expression Phillip had heard the others say when they left school at four in their clusters.

★

His grandmother and mother had escaped Germany with very little, just the belongings they could bundle in the lace cloth. Displaced, unable to grasp her new language or explore the bombed wastelands, they clung to the four o'clock ritual. After baking all day, thick, black coffee was brewed as the clock struck the hour. It grew weaker as the years passed. His grandmother reminded him daily she couldn't afford to run out.

"I imagined I would find English people reserved, but kind, strolling along verges and raising their hats to one another with unfailing politeness," she told Phillip often, always speaking in German. "But they are tired from the war. We all are."

Grandmother never saw Quiston Avenue and its dignified guard of genuflecting limes. After the funeral, she never left her flat.

Phillip went nowhere else, apart from school and the delicatessen in the alley on Saturdays. He should be there now, beneath the mottled, waxy cylinders of sausage suspended from hooks, breathing their smoky, choking stench.

His grandmother tasted freedom when the creamy chalk of Dover loomed. Its essence soaked the grey slab of the home that finally encased her while the possessions from her homeland became a reminder of the fear she had left behind.

"Freedom is inside these walls," she told her grandson.

★

Phillip tossed his cigarette into a puddle and walked to the royal-blue door. He stepped back a few paces and admired its immaculate sheen, its glorious colour, the paved steps leading up to it.

He could have been Julie's neighbour, rather than her guest, laughing with her every day over the back garden fence while they heaved in the laundry for their mothers. He could have heard her music through the wall. Even her anxious, irregular breathing when she had bad dreams at night.

Phillip cried for the first time while the rain banged on his leather jacket, making the same sound as the football vibrating the rounders shed, or the weary youth's head that soaked the wall outside their flat with blood from his brain.

"As long as no one intrudes," his grandmother said, sending Phillip out with a wet cloth. "As long as our door stays locked and it is just you and I here, Phillip, then we shall survive."

Faces might loom behind the nets of Quiston Avenue, but Phillip wouldn't see them. They didn't exist. It was just Phillip and his five-year-old self standing together, soaked and bruised like old blossom in a wet garden, not even waiting to be gathered up. Just staying forever where they fell.

He remembered the whiteness of the hospital; the white bandages and white nurses and white cups of milk. Doctors watched him, waiting for questions about his mother and father.

But Phillip said nothing. He just drank the milk and slept while his little bones healed. Then they took him to his grandmother's flat. He arrived at four o'clock in the afternoon and sat at the table with the cream and the silver. He discovered the sharp flavour of plum and the softness of fine cotton resting on his thighs.

He'd taken in a deep breath, so he could try to remember what the flat smelt like while he was at school and always let it welcome him home.

And in the dusk of Quiston Avenue, he turned round, passed through the lime corridor and headed for the alley. He would watch the butcher slice the cured meat for his grandmother, who waited in her mint dress for him to come home.

THE BIOLOGY LESSON

It was towards the end of the late afternoon Biology lesson, when Graham Robinson began breastfeeding.

He left his stool and gathered up the educational baby from the bench below the window, one hand supporting her neck. He sat down, her plastic head nestled in the crook of his left arm. Her legs lolled in their ink-stained rompers, so he curled his fingers around them to give support. Her ancient joints creaked in the silence.

Graham slipped the knot of his tie and undid his shirt. He leant forward until his nipple pressed onto her mouth. Rocking from side to side, he hummed a lullaby, a little cracked and out of tune, owing to his recently-broken voice.

The class gasped, as though Mr Lobb had told them the human heart was made of glass.

Mr Lobb frowned, his square glasses flashing. He gave Janine Rowe a sheaf of papers printed with questions for homework.

"Take one and pass them on, Janine," he said, glancing at Graham, then at his watch.

Graham transferred the infant to his other arm, murmuring 'Hush-A-Bye Baby'.

The semi-circle of pupils looked down at their sheets, the crowns of their heads almost angelic, shining under the strip-

99

lights. Blonde, brown, mouse, ginger. The only face visible to Mr Lobb belonged to Graham Robinson. Impassive, immobile, apart from the vibrations of his Adam's apple.

The bell rang with end-of-day finality. Mr Lobb raised his voice to warn about the complexity and urgency of the homework. Stools scraped. Papers rustled. Every eye turned to Graham.

Mr Lobb opened the door. The science lab filled with the corridor-echo of heels, triumphant Friday voices and steel lockers squeaking open, slamming shut.

Graham lifted the baby up to his shoulder, patting her back.

"Come on, Five B. No homes to go to? Move it, now. Not you, Graham."

As the door closed on the last shuffling pupil, Graham heard their rumble of conversation punctuated with shrieks. Mr Lobb busied himself with stacking stools until the noise faded. Graham put the doll back on the bench, folding a flopping arm across her chest, and watched trousers, skirts and blazers stream by, a long grey and navy smudge across the window.

"So Graham, rather a strange display, wasn't it?"

"Yes, Sir."

The teacher leant against the sink. Test-tubes tinkled on the draining-board.

"Everything all right with the revision? Stressed at all?"

"It's fine. I re-did the diagram of the ovaries. It made a difference, what you said."

Buses rumbled along the road, brakes wheezing.

"Remind me, Graham, could you? I don't recall..."

"You said I should sharpen my pencil, Sir. To make the labelling clearer."

Graham knotted his tie and pulled on his blazer. "Sir, my bus will be leaving in five minutes."

Mr Lobb removed his glasses. Graham saw the purplish dents they left on his cheeks.

"All well at home, Graham?"

"Yes. Absolutely, Sir."

Mr Lobb fished in his pocket and offered Graham a mint.

"And no one's dared you to pull infantile stunts in class?"

"Stunts, Sir?" Graham said, frowning.

"I'd not be surprised if Alan Lloyd or Terry played the fool, for instance. But you, Graham? You aren't really the sort."

Graham agreed with a nod. The Mint Imperials clacked on their teeth. Mr Lobb peeled off his white coat and bundled it into a cupboard.

"You can talk to me any time, Graham, rather than feel out of step with things," he said, polishing his glasses with a rag. He replaced a model of the human kidney on a shelf. "How are you feeling at the moment?"

"I'm not sure, Sir." Graham considered the question, but the answer slid like frog-spawn through his fingers.

They listened to the clock-hands for a full minute. Mr Lobb switched off the lights while Graham closed the top windows with the long pole. They exchanged polite, mannish smiles as they left, the teacher's green eyes still troubled when they shrank behind his thick glasses.

Graham sat at the back of the bus. Janine Rowe kept glancing at him from across the aisle. He watched her profile, the sweep of her hair along her jaw. He imagined running his finger along its blonde curve, then into the dip of her upper lip and along the lower lip that reminded him of a strip of raw steak.

He had seen Alan kiss her, mouths like desperate fish, fingers interlocking. Graham would hold her in his arms if he ever had the chance and touch his lips to her eyelids. He would lay his cheek against hers, just where her lashes could graze it. He wished he could just climb inside her and disappear.

He looked away, sensing the scornful gape of her mouth and her glassy blue eyes watching him.

On Fridays, a trio of women with their children caught his bus. They struggled on with folded pushchairs and quilted bags, still settling their babies as the driver pulled away. Graham folded his arms on top of the seat in front to watch.

"Will's quiet now, look," said the mother with nervous hands. "He was in such a state in the dry-cleaning shop. Over-tired, poor lamb. Awful night with his teeth."

"I could hear him when I was in Prior's ordering the birthday-cake," said the short mother with sensible curls.

"No, *could* you?" Will's mother bit her lip and smoothed her dozing son's hair.

"Emma loves 'Pat-a-Cake'," said the polo-necked mother. "It stopped her crying in the queue at the greengrocer's."

They sang a hushed version, tapping their hands on their children's listless fingers. Now and again, they looked round at their fellow passengers to see if they had an audience.

Graham rested his chin on his arms, listening. They talked of winter duffles and mashed bananas and non-slip slippers. They discussed Emma's first birthday. Red and yellow toys were poking from their carrier bags.

When they clattered off at the white gates of the new estate, Graham used his cuff to clear a patch on the clouded window. He smiled at them through the oval he had made, but they were hurrying away.

Janine banged him with her schoolbag when she climbed off at her stop. He watched her stroke a ginger cat on a wall. As her hand slid from its head to the tip of its tail, Graham's spine prickled from nape to tailbone.

Arriving home, he kicked the dying apples off the path. Most of them were infested with wasps that buzzed with anger as the fruit was buried in the long grass. His mother stood at the ironing board in the kitchen, listening to the radio. She put a finger to her lips. The play was reaching its climax. Unrestrained piano music and syrupy voices melted into unrestrained voices and syrupy piano. Then back again, as true love ran its course.

Graham's mother pointed at the fridge. He reached in and took the slice of meat pie up to his room.

He passed the spare bedroom, pausing to listen to the shallow, rapid breathing. The two sets of breath didn't synchronise today. As one inhaled, the other exhaled. He went to his own room and turned on Led Zeppelin as loud as he dared.

He spread his Biology books open beside his plate. He scraped his pencil point with a penknife and watched the grey flecks scatter across the pastry. He began to draw the meeting between sperm and egg.

Graham's music was too loud, his mother shouted on her way to the waking children. He paused his 'Stairway to Heaven', listening to their babble while she paced in silence around their mattresses on the floor. The doorbell chimed. Graham drew a smiling face on the egg and a moustache on the sperm.

"Thank you, Mrs Robinson," said the parents at the door, when his mother finally answered it. "What would we do without you?"

Graham heard their car drive away, the children strapped in. At home, the parents would wonder why bedtime was fractious. Tapping keyboards all day in pin-stripes and pencil skirts, they would want their glass of wine, their carton of frozen dinner. Want to dissect their triumphs and disasters. Murder and dismember colleagues over the coronation chicken. But their children would refuse to settle.

The dinners would dry as they toiled in turn, up and down the stairs, unaware that Mrs Robinson settled their babies to sleep all afternoon with matted teddies and bottles of sugared milk.

Graham heard the swish of his father's cheap windcheater, his mother's legs sliding into long zippered boots and their flat murmurs.

"Back later," they said.

"Bye," Graham muttered, turning on the music again.

They left to catch the bus for cribbage. The door rasped shut.

Graham went downstairs to his mother's cheap fragrance and his father's lingering last belch from his pub lunch. He spoke his name to the mirror to hear how he sounded. He didn't recognise his voice, low and gravelly, with an occasional croak. He put his face to the glass and watched it disappear behind a cloud of his breath.

Later tonight, the bed in the room beside his would groan. The shiny nylon bedspread would slide to the floor, slithering like snakes writhing on satin. Fridays were the days for love in Graham Robinson's house.

"Out-of-character behaviour," Mr Lobb would say in Monday's call to Mrs Robinson. "Exam pressure, peer pressure? Surely you've noticed something? Too little sleep, too much sleep? Sleepwalking, sleep eating, too many potato crisps? Any clues? Graham's not class clown material. Not like him at all. A phase, do you think?"

He would try to worm answers from her. She would sit in the kitchen with the telephone receiver. The curly wire would stretch so thin from its base in the hall every coil would disappear. She would still be wearing her nylon dressing-gown. A cup of tea and a dress catalogue would perch on her quilted lap while eggs for his father were jiggling in the poacher.

"Some rubbish about Graham acting odd," she would say afterwards, arranging the eggs on the plate with the striped rim. "Playing with a doll or something."

"It'll just have been a dare from one of the others. He's a mouse in school," his father would reply.

"Two rounds, Jim?" Mrs Robinson would ask. And he would nod and turn up the volume on the radio for the sports news.

Graham returned to his room and spread out his drawings. He

put his egg and sperm beneath the glow of his angle poise lamp and watched them merge. Another new life was beginning, the cycle spinning once more. He felt grateful for Mr Lobb's advice. A sharper pencil made all the difference.

He checked through his stack of old foetuses. Charlie at eleven weeks' gestation. Tillie at fifteen. Some fully coloured in. Others with meticulous shading and labels. A few twins. Once he felt satisfied they were still perfect, he tucked them into a plastic folder.

He switched off the lamp and prepared for bed, his day complete after the nightly ritual. All the children were safe, all within the early foetal stage where pain could not be felt.

Aurora and the Book Trolley

Sandra hoped the child would lose interest in her soon.

"I don't like being stared at," she murmured once or twice, although it took no notice.

Three nurses darted along the corridor, a fleeting distraction, but still it seemed to watch her.

Sandra wandered to the window. More nurses scurried like white ants in the courtyard. Plumes of smoke rose in the distance.

Sandra felt the child brush against her coat. It wore jeans and a lime jumper speckled with snags. Its hair was long and probably crawling. Sandra had heard it scratching.

A draught disturbed its enormous earrings. They creaked like chandeliers hanging by a thread in a bombed-out ballroom.

It looked like a feminine boy, but the earrings indicated girl. Who could be sure with those people?

It spoke. "What are you doing?"

"Looking outside. And you?" Sandra was polite, as if answering a query in the library. *Reference? Just along there on the next shelf, madam.*

"Waiting," answered the child.

"Well, that makes two of us."

Sandra paced, hoping to shake it off, but it followed, step for step.

"What are you, a doctor?"

"No. A librarian."

"Were you in the fire?"

"I don't look burnt, do I?"

"I don't know. My mum was. I'm waiting for her to be bandaged. The nurses sent me here because they don't know what to do with me. They said there were books. On a trolley."

"Ah yes," Sandra said. "The infamous invisible trolley. I'm waiting to restock it."

They sat down again, the child so close she could smell fried food in the fibres of its coat. Squeaking broke the silence.

"What's that?"

"It's the mobile library. *Words on Wheels*."

"Wow."

"Exactly."

The porter rammed the trolley into the wall at an angle. He panted, hands on hips, to let Sandra know this was not really his job.

"Choose a book to read if you like," Sandra said to the child. "I've got to take some back and replenish the trolley from my box."

She had no idea why she was being so amiable. Maybe because reading would keep the child quiet and stop it gazing at her.

"Why does everyone want to give me a book?" the child said. It inhaled loudly. "The paramedic, the triage man, the casualty nurse, the receptionist, the porter. Now you."

Sandra wanted to say, "Right miss, or sonny, whichever you are, let's get something straight here. No one's giving you anything."

But she supposed it had no notion of libraries, so she tried to be patient. "You can't keep a book. You can borrow one while you're here, but you must leave it on the trolley when you go home. Understand?"

107

"I like words."

"Jolly good. Take your pick while I sort out which to pack."

The child sat still while Sandra set to work.

"What's that smell?" it asked, wrinkling its nose.

"It's my disinfectant spray. I take it you've never seen one before." Sandra continued squirting and rubbing the plastic covers.

"Are the books germy?"

"Yes, they are. This stuff gets rid of bacteria."

"My name's Aurora."

"Well at least I can categorise you as a girl now," Sandra muttered, realising Aurora must be from the blazing sink estate. They probably all had fanciful names. The place must be chock-a-block with these scrawny, filthy Cinderellas, Rapunzels and Esmeraldas.

A huddle of nurses swept by. Their starched uniforms fanned the smoke filtering in from the estate.

"Are you going to choose a book?"

"Can't read."

"Ah. I see."

Sandra began classifying. She piled up the books with turquoise dots on the spine. They had been on the trolley long enough. She ticked them on her list. Six missing. She rummaged through again, but she was definitely short of three thrillers, two annuals and a Georgette Heyer. She frowned and circled the titles in red ink.

"Because I'm blind."

Sandra dropped the pen.

"What was that noise?" the child asked.

"I just dropped something. I'm sorry, Aurora. I didn't know you couldn't see."

"Do you have audio books?"

"I'm afraid not. Not with me."

Sirens howled through the wind. A white blur of doctors streamed by.

"My mum's going to be ages, isn't she? She's all burnt."

"I don't know, Aurora."

Sandra thought she heard the clotted sound of tears welling in the throat. She couldn't quite identify it. It might be hoarseness from the smoke or maybe that was the way the child talked, but while Sandra's words were still hanging in the silence, she realised the catch had been in her own voice.

★

Sandra had once marinated in tears because of Craig. Pickled in Craig-acid. That was the only time. She emerged from its vinegary horror an embittered, sharp and solitary librarian. It was the perfect arrangement. Not even the softest-centred love-stories induced weeping.

And Craig was diminished in stature from a broad and bearded Scot to a shoe box casting a small shadow on the garage wall.

It was vital to consign things to the right place. His clothes in a case he had paid for. His personal possessions in a strong container, so the bottom wouldn't fall out. His letters on the fire.

Their bed came apart with ease. Sandra re-flat-packed it, hired a van and drove it to the tip. A man offered to help, but her glare forced him back. She threw in the base sections first, then the mattress.

Finally she hurled in the head-board she'd heard clattering against the wall the day she came home early from work.

Craig had taken many years from Sandra. They could never be returned.

A few reminders of the marriage and its broken dreams remained in the shoe-box. Ranked *Archive*.

★

No, Sandra couldn't abide tears. She preferred to restore order.

"Do you know about the Dewey Decimal System, Aurora?"

The earrings clanked from side to side.

"Well, it chops all the stuff in the library books into ten classes. Each class is cut up into ten divisions. So there's a hundred of those. Then each one is split into ten sections. A whole thousand of them. Then all the books can be kept in the right order on the shelves."

"Do you like it?" Aurora asked, sitting forward, her chin jutting. "You sound all happy."

"Well, yes. I love it actually," Sandra said, moving across to Aurora's bench and sitting on the other end of it. "I like to know where I am with things. It makes my job in the library easy. Except when people put books back in the wrong place."

"That makes you cross, doesn't it?"

"Well, a bit vexed by the disorder."

"Cross, then."

"It's just that I'm better with things in their right place. I don't like being caught out."

"I think catching people out is good."

"Why on earth would you think that?" Sandra asked, inching closer.

"Well, because it shakes them up. Makes them think. I mean, there's thirty-five in my class. Half of them as thick as babies. Miss Ford says I'm the only one with an imagination. She never knows where she is with me. In Blackheath, or a black hole. Could be anywhere." Aurora swung her feet as she spoke, as if to emphasise her point.

Sandra edged nearer to focus on the child's eyes, now closed in concentration. "Shouldn't she give you work for an older age-group? Something to challenge you?"

"You're joking!" Aurora tossed her head back to face the suspended ceiling. "Her feet don't touch the ground. She's flying round the desks showing them how to hold a pencil. Or telling them what c-a-t spells."

"That can't be right," Sandra said, shaking her head. "Still, it must be tricky to teach unsighted children. Braille must take an age to master. Can't any of you see anything at all?"

Aurora shook her head at the false ceiling. "Some can a bit. I'm the only actually blind one. I see more in my head than they do though."

Sandra nodded, lost for words.

"If I was a book, where would you put me?" Aurora said, seeming to look into Sandra's eyes.

"Don't be silly! You can't file people!" Sandra stood up and began emptying the trolley.

Relieved of the final burden, its little wheels rolled towards Aurora. She grasped the handle and stepped onto the lower shelf.

Gathering speed, she skimmed along the corridor, whooping. At the end, before discovering the fixed wheels refused to turn corners, she sailed with great finesse into her mother's padded coat.

"Oh there you are, Lizzie," Aurora's mother said. "The twins have been checked out now. They kept us waiting ages."

Sandra dropped *Perfect Parenting*, a well-thumbed manual. It smacked onto the hard floor.

"Here you go." Aurora's mother picked up the book and put it on a pile of teenage angst. "Lizzie been keeping you company? All these books will have been the attraction. Blasted things. They're what give her this blooming over-active mind, as her teacher calls it."

Sandra could only nod.

"I'm forever falling over the piles of them in her room," the child's mother continued. "My other girls have dress-up clothes and such, but Lizzie won't play let's-pretend. Well, not in that way." She gathered the tiny hands of two toddlers, one on each side.

"This awful fire just missed our block. I wanted the boys checked though. They were coughing like mad from all the smoke."

"And you were hurt yourself," Sandra said.

"No, I wasn't. Like I said, it missed us, love. We're the lucky ones."

"It must have been frightening for Aur...er, Lizzie. Not being able to see, I mean."

"No, love. We're all fine. We could still see our way. Thinner smoke down our end." Lizzie's mother had raised her voice a tone by now and was looking at Sandra as if she might be a little deaf. Or a tad unhinged.

"Her eyes are all right then?" Sandra watched Aurora as she asked the question.

"Hang on," said the mother, her mouth alternately gaping and pursing like a startled fish. "No, don't tell me. I know what it is. It's that damn medical encyclopaedia again. Sorry, love. Lizzie muddles up her facts and her fiction." She lowered her voice to a hiss in Sandra's ear. "Does it on purpose, her teacher reckons. To get attention and reaction."

"Oh," Sandra said faintly.

"It's like an illness," the mother confided with pride, "but it's her way of reaching out to people. Otherwise, she'd be one of those sad types. Wasting her time with her nose stuck in a book all bloody day, never looking up. She had the triage nurse thinking she's got abdominal aortic aneurysm."

"Working through alphabetically. You'd approve of that," Aurora whispered to Sandra.

"Wait until you reach H," Sandra said with a smile.

"Why?"

"You'll be able to suffer hypochondria. Legitimately."

They moved apart while a stretcher rolled between them.

"All these poor burnt people," said the mother, clicking her tongue on the roof of her mouth. "No deaths, but their lives upside down. They couldn't save anything. I'll send them what clothes and bedding I can spare and I've got a cheese-pie made..."

She couldn't speak any more. She was trembling, her face waxy from the shock of being saved.

"Won't you sit down for a moment?" Sandra said. "I could try to find you a glass of water."

But the mother shook her head, pulling her children closer. She stuffed one of the little boys into Lizzie's arms and turned away, ready to go back to the home that was still standing.

As Sandra reclaimed her trolley, she listened to their fading conversation.

"Are those my earrings, Lizzie?"

"That's classified information, Mum."

At the end of the corridor Lizzie spun round to wink. Tucked under one arm was a book of fairy-tales.

Sandra laid her hands on the trolley and thought about the tiny knitted bootees in the shoe box in the garage. Peach, lemon and white. Assembled in order of colour and size. Soft as melted butter. Wrapped in velveteen layers of tissue. She could still feel the hopeful softness of the new wool and hear the silent paper membranes drifting into place as she packed them. She remembered the gouging, fruitless pain when she boxed them up unlabelled.

No point in keeping them. And the terraces of that estate were stacked with naked babies now, their routines in disarray. She would take the box down for people to sort through.

Sandra pushed the trolley to the side, leaving it in a neat parallel to the wall, and went home to make a start.

The Revival of Clara Petacci

When the fog on the platform thinned to reveal the cluster of commuters, Neil saw Clara Petacci. The insistent sun scorched her black curls and lit up her profile.

Neil moved a step closer. Everyone else melted into a cheerless solution, like old painting water in a jar. Neil had only to wade through them to reach Clara, touch her white face and bring his lips to hers.

He willed her to notice him. But nothing distinguished Neil. He wore grey like everyone else. His hair was the same short beige as other men waiting at Becontree for the nine o'clock fast train.

Amanda was at his elbow, pressing him about egg-salad or prawn.

"Prawn, then," he answered, feeling her impatience.

A cloud coasted over the sun. He couldn't see Clara Petacci now.

"Prawn? At eight forty-five? I thought you'd save it for lunch and have the egg now," Amanda said.

Neil scanned the crowd.

"What are you looking for, Neil? Take your egg. You're as white as a sheet, for heaven's sake."

The express blasted through like a silver wind.

"Lord alive, Neil!" Amanda shouted, catching hold of him with one square, capable hand. "Get a grip. We're only going to choose the ring, not face a firing squad."

Neil tried to fit the dislodged sections of his day together. The picture had looked clear a few minutes ago until Clara was painted into it.

A day free from college gave Neil a scrap of deliverance from the jumble and clutter of history. But he fretted about his freedom just as he did when he played pool alone, cracking in the black when he knew he should be hunched over a book in the arid peace of the library.

Tutorials tortured him. Dry dates, polemics, the rigmarole of royalty and reign. It all induced a sweat of confusion, sealing Neil to his seat in the ring of chairs around the professor.

But the tutorial-trio thrived; the blonde girl with clear, mauve eyes, the tall boy with skin like spotted-dick and the earnest ginger lad with soggy lips. They answered and asserted. They sorted and sifted the facts that writhed in Neil's head. He rehearsed the words he hoped to slot in, but they mutated into butterflies that fluttered and panicked, struggling to escape, finally pinning themselves flat inside his mind.

History sprang up inside him, but it stayed there. The others couldn't see it and Neil couldn't elucidate it for them. History didn't come to life for him as it did for the others in Room 22A.

He looked at Amanda's sure-footed body, her legs apart like a divided tree-trunk, arms folded beneath the smug bosom that would soon loom and hover over his face, harpooning his head to the pillows of the London Traveller Hotel.

He took a gulp of the sun-laced air, struggling to clarify his thoughts. He was catching a train with Amanda to buy their engagement ring. She'd said they must get rolls. She felt faint with hunger. The cornflakes at her flat had gone soft. Neil hadn't folded the paper innards over them enough times. And they had to buy extra rolls ready for lunch because there would be nowhere cheaper than Becontree.

She wanted the blue and white cubic zirconium, three stones. She had a voucher for free coffee afterwards in the London Traveller Hotel. She wanted them to sneak into a vacant bedroom for half an hour and giggle at the jangle and clang of approaching chambermaids. Amanda savoured the risk of discovery.

But Neil didn't feel like taking risks. He prayed she wouldn't make that yodelling noise. He imagined the porter whipping the quilt away, thrusting Neil into the stripe of daylight that always jived between hotel curtains. Amanda planned to wear the purple camisole rolled up in her bag. She couldn't put it on in the flat. It was too tight under her arms for travelling.

Neil wanted to sit on the bench and wait for the train. He could watch the crowd disperse into queues at each carriage until only Clara remained, beckoning him.

The tannoy gargled. Men listened, squinting at the announcement about the train, then draped their jackets over briefcases and snapped glances at their watches. The sun flared as they paced, measuring the damage of the delay to their schedules.

Neil would rather go to the stationery shop than the jeweller. He needed ring-binders to keep his shambolic notes intact. The clear-eyed blonde shortened each session to bullet-points. Her nail tips scampered over cards in a tiny index file. Blasts of black biro spotted the edge of each card. Blam, blam, blam.

Amanda cut through his thoughts. "Neil, come on, the train's going to be late. Might as well sit in the waiting room."

"Won't it be hot in there? And crowded?"

"Neil, I'm not standing here for an hour." Amanda's hair hung in strings around her boiled-potato face. Neil pulled away. He could see Clara's wide mouth. It was like a fresh-cut slice of peach.

"What's wrong with you now?" Amanda said. "Have your egg roll, look. You're looking all pasty."

She stood there, crumbs cascading to the ground. Neil longed to push her aside, his stomach churning with guilt. She was unwrapping his breakfast for him. Egg-shreds crawled from their doughy cell.

"Amanda," Neil said, "do you know Mussolini's mistress?"

"Christ, Neil. You know I don't like war films."

"No. No, I don't mean a film. I mean the real woman."

"Jesus, Neil. I don't know you at all today. Have you overdosed on your hay-fever tablets again?"

Amanda's voice drilled into him like a woodpecker on speed. She pecked at his surface, never piercing the pulp of his soul.

He wanted rain to empty the platform of people. He would edge closer to Clara, until he could see the droplets quiver in her hair.

New crowds heaped up on the platform to wait for the next train. They swallowed Clara. Neil searched, pushing past backs and bags and feet and flanks.

Amanda tugged the sleeve of his sweater. "For God's sake, Neil. Where are you going?"

Another express vibrated the track. A swarm of commuters nudged Neil and Amanda near the edge of the platform. His foot inched over the yellow danger-line.

It would be easy to fall. Clara would already be kneeling on the track. Her arms would catch him. "Hush," she would whisper. He would lay his cheek against the vanilla skin of her neck. The sun would rupture through the cloud. He'd trace his finger between the fragile bones on the back of her hand. They'd smile as the train approached, their passion powerful enough to confront it.

He watched the express inject itself into the station, a poison flushing through the track. His foot was over the lip of the platform.

Amanda gripped his elbow. The cold rush in his ears almost drowned her curses.

"Jesus Christ, Neil, you're an absolute enigma today. Look, come back from the edge, will you? Come *on*. You almost had us on the bloody track. Who the *hell* were you looking for?"

"I told you, Amanda. Mussolini's mistress. Her name is Clara Petacci. Pale as lilies. Dark hair. Taller than you."

"And she's actually here, this Clara, is she?"

"Somewhere. She came from Giulino di Mezzegra."

"To Becontree?"

"Yes. But I can't see her at the moment. I'm afraid you're putting her off."

Amanda shook her head, peering at Neil. "Neil, who the bloody Hell is this Clara?"

"The perfect woman, Amanda."

Neil and Amanda were in everyone's way. They had to turn towards the refreshment room. He saw a woman in rose pink among the crowd. She looked in his direction and he strained towards her, but Amanda tugged him inside.

They sat down at a table littered with remains. Neil tried to decipher them, turning the crumbs and crusts into an untouched meal in his mind.

Amanda took her purse out to buy tea. She fiddled with the catch, as if she were trying to locate words to match her thoughts. Neil imagined her brain writhing like laundry in a machine, unused to the muddled load Neil had deposited there.

She took off her cardigan, revealing a new green blouse. Too small, as usual, Neil noticed. But today the pale sprigs of daisies printed on it made her seem almost fragile, rather than over-stuffed like the arms of an aunt's sofa. He thought about her typing all day at Horlock-Fenny Sprockets, counting every penny, so Neil could be free to study. But Amanda provoked only thoughts, rather than feelings.

"I love Clara, you know," he said.

Amanda was silent. Her purse thumped onto the table.

"We're self-service here, you know," a waitress barked.

While Amanda watched Neil, the door rattled open, over and over again. People reeking of hasty cigarettes and cheap body spray scraped their shoes on the mat. The queue at the counter shuffled in silence. A man in fur frowned at the limp bacon rashers drowning in their own fat. A woman with a shopping-basket on wheels read a novel as she waited for her tea. Urns hissed and bread-slices browned. Neil picked at his fingernails.

Zirconium forgotten, Amanda stared at an abandoned currant in a pool of butter. "So who is she, Neil?" she said at last. "And what's Mussolini got to do with the price of fish? Some kind of code or what?"

"It's just that Clara and I know the power of love," Neil said.

"Neil, our ring is sitting in a red suede box at Belcher & Barnes," Amanda said. "We're in love. And we've paid our deposit." Her voice retained its usual tautness, but her eyes glittered.

"Amanda," Neil whispered, his words almost lost among cups crashing onto saucers and emptied trays banging down on the stack, "would you shield me with your body if someone aimed a gun at me? That's what Clara did. Would you sacrifice your life to try to save me, even if I were the most evil man in the world? It's the measure of love. Would you do it?"

Amanda whispered back. It was a sound Neil had never heard before. He didn't know this Amanda, quietly in flames.

"Neil, what's your current module about? Is it dictators?"

Dictators sounded worse when it was whispered. Neil nodded, upturning the sugar and trailing a granular serpent across the Formica.

"I'm guessing Clara tried to protect Mussolini when they were executed," she said. Neil nodded again, tracing through the sugar-snake, leaving gaps in the curving line.

"Neil, Clara is a ghost. You can admire her gesture, but she won't be able to buy you a cup of tea. Or tie you with a chiffon scarf to the trouser-press in the London Traveller. Or thank you with all her heart for the beautiful ring."

Neil couldn't explain that history was an awakening of love, the kind that would lay itself down and die.

Their train was due. They returned to the platform. Only a few passengers waited, pulling raincoats on as the sky darkened.

The woman in the pink suit hurried onto the platform, her thin legs whisking back and forth like scissors snipping, asking if the train had gone yet. Neil moved towards her. Amanda put out her hand to stop him.

"Neil, she isn't Jackie Kennedy."

Neil looked at the woman with her back to him. He looked at her dark-brown, motionless hair and graceful limbs. His dear Jackie. She loved every part of him with such purity that, when the sniper attacked, she would collect fragments of his head from the seat of the train.

The pink lady was unzipping her briefcase. Neil stiffened.

"It's all right, Neil. If she's got a gun, I promise I'll fling myself in front of you. All right? Now get the sherbet-pips out."

Jackie wouldn't fire a gun. Amanda knew nothing.

Clara appeared beside Jackie. She waited, a newspaper under one arm. Two women, intact from the vat of history, unsullied by the reams of dates and dusty facts that teemed in his head. Excavated from bloody soil, brushed down by his own trembling fingers. History in flesh. Love revived.

The leash of learning had loosened around Neil's neck. History was coming out. He could feel its tissue. He could grind it, knead it and trap it under his nails. It yielded to his bite, nourishing him with the blood of sacrificial love.

He was free. He didn't need ring-binders. He had dug out the past with bare determination. And here it was, laid open on Becontree Station. If only the professor could see how far he'd come.

Neil looked at Jackie's hand clenching the piece of brain. Amanda would say it was a plastic coffee-cup.

"I know I should trust you, Amanda," he said. "But not to do so will be much better."

He snatched her bag and rummaged in it for the knife he'd wrapped in her camisole.

"Stab me," he said.

She took the knife. It flashed in her hand.

The two women would shield him from Amanda. Clara would deflect the blade and Jackie would absorb it into her heart. Or perhaps vice versa. One way or another, they would leave Neil absolutely whole. Amanda would be taken away, while he knelt by the corpses and whispered his gratitude before burying them back in the past.

But it was Amanda's voice he heard in his ear, saying she would take him home.

MICHAEL'S LIST OF FEARS

Relieved it was early and the queues in the departure-lounge short, Frances bought a cardboard sandwich and coffee. She peeled back the cellophane, while Michael watched her hands shaking. She rushed back to find a plate. He had come to loathe casual eating and learnt to prefer a cloth on the table and the right crockery. She had once served him a round of toasted cheese on a vast dinner plate. He couldn't eat it. Said it looked lost.

While holidaying families in pineapple-prints and coconut lotion filed past, jolting their chairs, Frances sipped her tea and watched Michael eating. He didn't look up.

At dawn she had touched his hair. He had woken quickly. Kissed her slowly. They had not spoken. The room was sprayed with end of summer rain from the open window.

★

Last year, he had slipped like winter sun into her guest house. Since the children had left, with Roger slinking off soon after, there were too many swollen rooms and well-fed plants. Her echoing home demanded a change. It was that, or cram all those years into a magnolia box.

She chose change and remoulded the family nooks into clear spaces, advertising it as a holiday-home.

Guests came for a few nights by the coast, sponging up salt air all day and sliding into her pressed sheets to dream of hot breakfasts. Frances became bed-maker and egg-fryer, seeking out her old apron and resigning herself to reeking of smoky lard all over again.

Michael prowled into the country, hungry like a lean cat seeking new hunting-ground. Eyes full of need, hair wild in the November wind. Framed in her doorway, he looked fragile. She asked him in before he blew away.

Michael was not his name, but it was the closest she could find to his unpronounceable real one. He had pencil-stubs and paper, but few clothes. His comb had nine teeth. He wore a bar of soap to a sliver in three days. She gave him the best room, next to her own at the far end of the landing.

Frances drove into town and bought shaving foam and razor-blades. She asked the assistant about suitable lipsticks for the middle-aged woman, laughing as she spoke, as if age were something to mock. But the assistant gave Frances's skin tone careful consideration and declared *Rampant Raisin* not too obvious a shade.

The art shop on the corner beckoned her inside. A kind of dream guided her to blocks of paper, palettes of water-colour, giant tubs of brushes and tins of pastels. She emerged into bright rain, nursing the full bag in both arms.

She sheltered the purchases under her coat, her hands pressing with pride on the swelling. Passing other windows, she spotted the reflection of her rounded shape.

The other guests dwindled and Frances put off callers. "I've closed for the winter," she said.

Michael came to her with sombre eyes and a penitent handful of coppers and she said he could wash her car instead of paying.

He approved of the northerly light in the dining room. It became his studio without him claiming or Frances offering it. He drew in the mornings, slept all afternoon and painted half the night.

Sometimes she would find him stretched on the carpet at dawn, wearing the baggy green cords Roger had left behind, his neglected coffee taut with skin. French-blue waves stiff with whipped-cream froth soared on the canvases Frances had bought him.

Michael pointed out the sandy-coloured grime wedged between the tiles in his shower. Frances showed him the new grouting in hers. He gathered his wash-kit.

His towel slithered off as he eased into the tiny cubicle, spare and brown and smelling of young man's skin. He whisked the curtain back to ask for soap. He didn't like gel. Frances fiddled with the paper casings of a new bar and handed it to him. The steam was relaxing her perm and shining her cheeks, but she didn't think about herself, even when she caught sight of her misted reflection in the mirror. She thought about the future instead.

Frances plunged into her sea of unused recipe-cards. She swam through Scotch Broth, dived down into the depths of Moroccan Tagine, climbed up banks of Chinese lychees and Greek almonds, and all the way back to the local fish market. Michael wolfed down some meals and stubbed his cigarette out in others. He talked all the time to improve his English and so that Frances could savour his intense, luscious accent.

One evening, she cleared the table in silence. He had pushed aside his plate of mangled snapper, lit a cigarette and started to draw on her serviette, a good Irish linen. Frances was still eating.

She watched him pour more wine for himself and suddenly felt terribly British. She collected his plate with her back half-turned and made a lot of clatter with the cutlery, hurling it into the dishwasher. She slammed it shut and gave it a kick, smashing her toe. She yelled with rage, although she knew as she raged that it wasn't Michael who had made her angry.

He bound the toe gently to the one next to it and drove her to the hospital. She knew he wasn't insured to drive, but her senses were fogged by the brandy he had fed her. All she noticed during the three-hour wait, was the olive corduroy of his trouser-leg touching her brown polyester. She felt so foolish, so old.

After that, he drove all the time. Sometimes by himself, disappearing for hours, and occasionally to take Frances shopping. At the supermarket, Michael explained he had never seen cows and pigs in packets before. He picked whisky for his nightcap and quail's eggs for a still-life. He stroked the tiny, speckled shells one by one, releasing them from their plastic bubbles and carefully replacing them. He discarded many boxes before making his choice. Aisle after aisle was explored and the trolley soon groaned from the weight of Michael's pleasures. He passed it to Frances and fetched a second one. She had to limp fast to keep up, her foot throbbing.

When she gave him his own key, he was so grateful he dashed straight to the dining room and fetched a few almost-finished watercolours. He presented them to her, holding the pictures between them like a new child.

She found the children's ancient picture books and taught him to read English. In order to practise, he wrote reams of lists. Always ten items per list. Colours, shapes, animals, vegetables, phrases for restaurants, for banks, for complimenting.

"You wear a very nice dress" he often told her, falling silent while he watched her face flush.

Making his bed one day, she found a list tucked under his sheet.

The heading, *Michael – List of Fears*, was scribbled in faint pencil. There were five entries.

Never be good artist.
Get fat like inglish mens.
Lose my hairs.
Hurt my hand.
Not sell my painting and have go back.

125

Frances reread it many times. Holding it to her face, she smelt it. She refolded it and opened it out again, peering between the words.

Of course his vocabulary was still limited, she reminded herself. The list was unfinished because he always wrote out ten things. There were more to come.

She put it back and smoothed it beneath the sheet, marbled with guilt. But she knew she would look again, greedy for his remaining fears.

Michael discovered pubs. All his lists became pub names, pub drinks and pub jokes. He made pub friends. They bought him whisky in return for his exotic company and beautiful face. One night, he brought a loud party home and shouted out to Frances, "Hey, we will have bangers!"

They all cheered and settled at the table.

"Bangers and mash, Frances," he called again, "on the green plates. There are enough, yes?"

She was in her candlewick dressing-gown, skin greased and the hair pins at her temples clinging onto today's curls in preparation for tomorrow. Tomorrow, Michael would celebrate a year in England. She had hidden a good sparkling wine in the fridge. The sausages were waiting for a picnic in the park. She had found the old hamper in the attic, full of the scent of old summers.

"Michael, those are for..."

"Oh, let us not be boring, Frances. Put them in a pan for us and go to bed. You are tired. Karen will cook."

Karen was bouncing beside him, poured into a white dress like a bottle of fresh milk.

As Frances unravelled the sausages, Michael wrapped himself around his dairy maid and laid his Scotch-soaked head on her full-cream breast.

Frances couldn't sleep. The smell of charred pork-fat slithered out of the kitchen, up the stairs and curled into her room. Later, the front door slammed several times amid lively departing voices. She counted the goodbyes. Not everyone left.

Out of bed, her ear to the door, she listened to the passion. From kitchen to living room, to the hall. Then up the stairs and along the landing to the room at the end, next to hers.

The anniversary passed in silence. Michael slept all day and Frances walked on the beach in the rain.

A few weeks later, the authorities caught up with him and told him to leave. With good cheer he packed all the things he had acquired. He rejected a suitcase. His battered holdall had accompanied him the world over and would root him to wherever he found himself.

He seemed passive about moving on. On the last night, he dismissed his friends, even Karen, without a backward glance, but Frances was shaking.

She went into his room at dawn and opened the window to let out the last stale waft of eau-de-cologne Karen had left behind.

She climbed in beside Michael like a child seeking comfort from a bad dream. She was trembling, frightened of waking him in case he shouted and ordered her out. Frightened of not waking him, in case this chance was lost.

Michael opened his eyes and gave her his slow, lazy smile, as if she might be a birthday present he had overlooked. She was unwrapped, admired, and, once the alarm clock broke their fusion, set aside and asked to run his bath.

She dashed to the shop for his cigarettes and came back to see him ready in the doorway. The spiteful wind had whipped up, ready to sift him away.

★

Just before the flight was called, he gave her a parcel containing three of his pictures; a sullen gull, a quail's egg with no shadow

127

and a rough sketch of Karen in a camisole. He also gave her a grubby piece of folded paper and asked her to open it.

"Now, please, Frances."

She stopped breathing. If he feared losing her, if her name was there on his list, in any capacity at all, then she would know. She would know she was doing the right thing.

It was an invoice.

"They are best work. Fair price for you, Frances."

"Yes, I'm sure, Michael."

"There is money-machine over there. Is working. I looked."

"Oh, right."

"Must do it now. Plane leave soon."

She pressed the numbers and slowly extracted the money. In this last bitter pocket of time, Frances paid the price.

She went home. She called his name and listened to the echo. When it faded, she called again and again until she was screaming into the emptiness, until her voice dried in her throat.

She could still smell him, as though he might materialise in the doorway, on the stairs, at the kitchen table. She walked from room to room. The echo of her tears followed, dogging every step.

She thought about the cliffs he had painted, impossibly white and jagged against a hopelessly indigo sky. She went to his cliffs one afternoon in a gale and looked down from the edge, but she saw no answer.

'For heaven's sake, Frances,' she told herself. 'What the hell were you expecting to do? You're wearing Roger's old oilskins and stout hiking-boots. And before you ventured out, you slipped the mini torch and a Wagon Wheel in your pocket. You've even left the pin-curlers in your hair under your sou'wester. You are programmed to be sensible. Pre-set to survive. Come on, you're hardly broken, are you? You meant all along to go back.'

She chose the only possible course of action with the house

too empty. She made a list. She wrote down the options and saw them all through.

She wrote invitations to her children, saying they should visit soon. She made an apple-pie for the freezer. She struggled with the dining table, inching it back into its normal position.

When she stripped Michael's bed, the list of fears fluttered into the air and settled in his ash-tray.

Frances reached into her apron pocket and pulled out her one-way ticket. She placed it on top of the list and glanced around her. He had left behind a matchbox containing one match.

When the flame died down, she cleared out the ash with all the rest of the debris. Her home wanted to be aired.

She went outside. A drift of cloud was exposing hints of weak blue. It might brighten up later. A few dozen gulls rose from the beach in a raucous huddle. As she watched them soar, they separated, wheeling and changing direction in glorious appreciation of their liberty.

THE ENGLISH LESSON

Someone once told Dieter that a heartbeat can slow down for one unsought second that takes cover in the memory like a hidden light. When one of these old lights emerges, connections with pain are severed. But when the heart gathers power again, the light retreats.

Dieter wished he could summon these memories at will, in the same way that his teeth sculpted each bite of cheap fruit-bread to contain at least one sultana, like a small burst of wine.

But the moments came unbidden.

In the language-assistant's room, Susan Brown was coaxing him through English tenses. Dieter could only concentrate on the green spears of gladioli she had arranged in a glass vase. Red buds were pushing through their caul of leafy skin, a blind passage into the air.

A football thumped against the wall outside, close to the window behind him. Dieter didn't duck. He felt the heat of hard eyes and suppressed laughter scorching his back. The ball scuffed the ground. The boys were placing it ready for the next kick, willing him to jerk like a puppet this time.

Miss Brown was looking through the window, not rapping on it like the normal teachers. She just murmured English words, then sealed her lips over her soft-looking teeth. Her skin was curd-white and her hair draped like brown lace over her shoulders. She seemed to have come here, not simply from another country, but from another age, an age of grace.

Dieter hoped she would keep him in her room until the last bus took the boys away at four thirty. The weak winter light would fade as they walked. She might wait for him while he bought the dry shreds of cooked meat for his mother. The street light would switch itself on as they talked. With the ham parcel cold in his hands and his satchel at his feet on the frozen ground, he would keep her there and tell her his sister was born yesterday. He would explain how he missed her so much he would like the butcher's cleaver to chop through his heart.

Susan Brown lived in a hostel, she had told Dieter. She spent her evenings writing letters to her fiancé in England, while the other young people fried eggs or played table-tennis. She wrote on sky-blue airmail paper. It rustled like onion-skins. He had seen her alone in this room at break time, covering leaf after leaf with her rounded, careful writing.

At the beginning of the year, her lips used to press a waxy imprint of her smile on the back of the envelopes. But last Saturday, he had seen her roller-skating in the park with the others from the hostel. One young man wreathed a long, scruffy scarf around his neck and hers, lacing them together. Dieter saw her shed her neat blazer and lay it over a tree stump.

She shook her head when the boys slammed the ball against the window frame. If the glass shattered, flakes of window would rain on Dieter's back like sugar crystals. But Susan Brown didn't shout for them to stop. They knew she wasn't a real teacher yet. She was just beginning.

"Before my journey with my mother this morning, I am drinking coffee with her in Hertie's store. That is why I come late," Dieter told Susan.

They listened to the wind scurrying the ball across the asphalt.

131

A flicker of sun lit the white veins of the compass-point scratches in Dieter's desk. With the point of his pencil, he stirred blotting-paper scraps in the ink well into a fountainhead of ink-speckled confetti.

The ball pounded against the window. Dieter couldn't help hunching over, clapping his hands over his head to the sound of shrieks and guffaws.

"Bloody thugs. No respect at all," Susan whispered, glaring at the boys. "How that glass didn't smash, I've no idea. In England, we'd be grinding it under our feet."

"Pardon, Miss Brown?" Dieter said, sitting up, noticing the angry blood rush into her neck.

"Never mind," she said. "Come and sit by me, out of the firing line. That's it. Excuse me a minute, Dieter, I'll shut that high window."

It took her a few attempts because she wasn't tall. The boys were shouting remarks. Dieter saw dark stains spread under her arms. Her hands were trembling. She looked lonely, as if she wanted to take the bus to the port and the next ship to Harwich. He imagined her curled in the recess of a port-hole, watching the sea take her away.

"Did you enjoy your breakfast in Hertie?" Miss Brown asked, sitting down again, the din of the footballers hushed now.

Dieter listened to the swish of her skirt lining against her stockings as she crossed her legs.

"It rains like ice when we are walking there," he said. "Nothing is for breakfast. We eat first rye-bread at home. We drink only coffee in Hertie because we are too soon for the hospital. We cannot…er…I don't know. Not time. Window is still closed. When we walk there, I hold my sister to my chest. My hand is like an umbrella for my sister's head. Her hair is thin. It is, how you say... silken."

Miss Brown smiled at him. "Your tenses need polishing, Dieter.

You should be using past tense. And you said 'window' instead of 'door'. 'Soon' instead of 'early'. But 'silken' is excellent. What is your sister's name?"

"Her name was Ilse."

"You should say 'is', Dieter. You don't need the past tense now, because Ilse is still her name. It's in the present time." Miss Brown eased her chair back.

"It was Ilse's last journey with us," he said.

The feet of Miss Brown's chair squealed on the floor. He wanted her to smile again, but her hand was over her mouth.

Dieter's heart was thudding the way Ilse's did on his lap in Hertie. Leaning over her, his face had brushed her chest. He felt her heart leap like a tiny fish inside his ear-drum. He sat up again, watching his red-raw wrists jabbing out of his worn cuffs. And then he saw how his fingers curved in a beautiful arc, cradling Ilse, keeping her safe from the scalding coffee and the damp shoppers passing their table.

"I'm so sorry, Dieter," Susan whispered. "Oh my goodness, you shouldn't be at school. Shall I walk you home?"

"It was a long journey," he said. "I want it not to begin. And Hertie was so very warm."

Susan was listening, searching his sentences for the truth, or perhaps for mistakes, like a dentist's hook probing for specks of decay.

He couldn't speak anymore. The room was inside a kaleidoscope. Red and green fragments were thrashing in the blackness around him.

"Dieter," Susan said, "are you all right?"

The electric heater in the corner spluttered, the orange bars fading, its warmth dying on Dieter's ankles. The scent of Miss Brown's summery perfume had strengthened in the heat. He was sealed in here with her, with the long gladioli towering over them like sentry guards. Her tapestry bag was filled, as always, with airmail paper and packets of liquorice cat-shaped sweets. Today, she had also brought a plastic bag that bulged with roller skates.

He rubbed at his eyes with his sleeve. "Yes, Miss Brown. I'm well. Er, will your fiancé meet you in England in summer?"

"Well, that's his plan," she said, looking down at her skirt.

"Will you see him from the ship in England?"

"Well I don't know about that, but he says he'll wait in the café on the docks with a pot of tea and a plate of scones," she said. "That's what he wants to do."

"Why?"

"To welcome me back English style, I suppose."

Dieter heard the lament of seagulls and smelt the salt air. He saw Miss Brown trying to locate her man among the damp coats and stacked luggage.

"And are you, how do you say, overjoyed for your wedding?"

Miss Brown often twisted her engagement ring round and round, letting it catch the light. Sometimes it slipped along her finger and almost came off, but today it wasn't there.

She didn't answer him.

★

This morning in Hertie, his mother tried to stretch the last few minutes. Her tongue probed her cup where a scab of sugar clung to a trace of coffee skin. When she took Ilse from Dieter, he wound and unwound his long scarf around his neck many times over, his hands restless. His mother waited. She gave Ilse a kiss. Normally, she would have sighed and asked him to hurry.

The waitress came, the one with the dewy mouth like morning rose petals. Dieter wondered how many times a day she repainted her lips so they always looked the same throughout her shift. He imagined her standing at the mirror, bringing her face to life.

"Another?" the waitress asked, reaching out a finger and tickling Ilse's chin with the tip of a polished fingernail.

Dieter raised his eyebrows at his mother and unwound his scarf, hoping they could stay longer.

"There is no time," she said, setting the cup down on the saucer without a sound.

They walked in step. His mother's pace was slow because she had given birth the day before. Her legs were tired. Her emptied belly swung under her coat.

Ilse had been born in their bath to avoid stains on the bit of carpet in the other room. Dieter wiped the bath and lino afterwards and laid the baby in an empty drawer, his anorak beneath her as a mattress. He hoped her cheek would touch the gentle furry lining in the hood.

Dieter tried to forget the purpose of their journey. The coffee swum in his stomach. His breath hung in the cold air. His heart was wrung dry like the salt-fish strung up in the harbour.

The journey was painful because of sudden hailstones. Dieter wrapped his scarf round his sister. They paused in the woods to shelter under a tree. His mother fed Ilse for the final time. Dieter's arms encircled them both, while hail rattled on the back of his jacket and his sister sucked and sucked, as if she would never taste milk again.

They arrived at the hospital window to find it locked. They walked around the courtyard for ten more minutes, while blackbirds heralded the sun. Lime leaves curled up to nurse the raindrops, but their weight and the wind slid them along the veins until they dropped from the tips, staining the ground.

The key rattled in the lock of the baby-window. They walked over to it. Dieter read the sign. *Babyfenster.*

If you leave your baby here, he will be looked after, no questions asked. If unclaimed after eight weeks, your child will be adopted. Why not leave a letter he can read in the future?

"It's better than out on the steps in this cold," his mother said, as if she referred to the delicate bay tree they had once owned.

After ten minutes, a sensor in the bed triggers an alarm, alerting the duty-nurse in the delivery room to the new arrival.

Dieter's mother asked him to open the window. It was actually a wooden hatch with a handle. There was no glass.

She placed Ilse in the small bed that was heated to thirty-seven degrees centigrade. She covered her with the lemon blanket, which was already turned back. Ilse wriggled and sighed, full of milk, protected from the bitter day.

His mother tried to close the hatch slowly, but it shot into place.

Dieter imagined the duty-nurse listening to the grind of their shoes in the gravel path. She might glance out and see their retreating shadows.

The sensor would respond any moment to Ilse's soft weight. Dieter clenched his fists. His fingernails stuck in his palms. His breath froze in the air. He felt winded, as if his mother had kicked a football into him.

He wished the boys from school would appear. With their knuckle-headed sense of justice they would force the hatch off its hinges. Their rough fingers would acquire finesse, unfolding the blanket, easing her out, cupping her head, bringing Ilse out into the world.

Dieter and his mother walked on.

They parted at the corner by the cooked-meat shop. She would go home to their flat for a sleep while Dieter hurried to school. She dropped a few pfennig into his hand to pay for the bits that always shed from the ham-joint hanging in the window.

"Buy the offcuts at the end of the day," she said. "They would only be swept up from the floor."

★

The football-players were leaving to catch their bus, shouting as they passed the window. Dieter imagined them going to their homes on the new estate where their mothers would slice sugar-crusty streusel weighed down with plums and sweetened with cream. And the boys would eat, the day forgotten, while their mothers wiped their hands on their aprons and switched on lamps.

"Stay for a bit, until the coast is clear," Susan Brown said, offering him a liquorice. "Um...is your little sister all right, Dieter? I'm not sure, you see, if we might have our wires crossed. You mentioned something about it being the last time..."

He shifted the liquorice cat to one cheek. It burned there, but he liked the bitter-sweet heat of it in his mouth

"She is well, Miss Brown."

"Oh, what a relief. I thought you meant...well, never mind now. I suppose we should make tracks soon. I must catch the post."

"A letter to England?"

"Yes. It must go today. I've spent days writing it."

"I'll post it for you, Miss Brown. The post-box is by the butcher."

"Thank you, Dieter. That would be a very kind favour. Make sure you do, won't you? Make sure it catches the post."

"I can watch for the postman to come, but..."

"What is it, Dieter?"

He imagined her running along the road, her cobwebby hair flailing, begging him not to post it. And his hand would be in the slot, the letter falling from his fingers like a leaf to join the pile inside.

"Nothing. Just...are you sure, Miss Brown?"

She nodded and handed it to him. He wished they could stay here, but the heater was out and she was switching off the lights.

The letter weighed nothing in Dieter's hands. He would have to hold and post it with care before the wind snatched it away. Then, just before the butcher slid his shutters down, he'd slip

137

inside the shop for the meat, his feet leaving their marks in the day's sawdust.

They went out into the icy afternoon. Miss Brown locked the door and jangled the keys into her pocket. She had left her tapestry bag behind. "I don't need it tonight," she said, hugging the plastic bag of skates. "There's nothing of value in there."

"When Ilse was born," he wanted to tell her before she walked on, "I knew I'd wait my whole life for something to equal that."

He had not spoken out loud, unsure of the right words in English for the past and present. There was probably no point in pinning down time in that way.

He could still feel Ilse's heavy head in the curve of his neck, as if she lay there now. He could see her mouth closing round her wrinkled fists. His own heart was pulsing inside her from the second she was born.

It was a pinprick of light, dancing like a firefly to its own tune. There was no time of arrival. But the memory was always waiting, hoping to hook up your pain and bring you a moment's peace. And there wasn't a language for that.

THE LONG DRIVE

Elizabeth opened the newspaper and spread it on Ralph's armchair

"There, dear," she said, patting it. "It's all ready for you to sit back down. You won't be sick now."

Ralph gave her a satisfied smile, his few ochre teeth poking out like sweetcorn kernels.

He thumped onto the seat, rustling the paper, and thrust out his arms to the dashboard.

"Must find my Ordnance Survey," he said, unhinging the glove compartment. The flap shot down and maps spilled out. He reached behind him.

"Is my cane on the back seat?" he asked.

"Yes, I'm sure it is, dear," Elizabeth reassured him. "On top of your sandwiches. With your Imperial Mints."

"Get back to it then, Elizabeth. I've stopped feeling car-sick. The newspaper trick is working."

He laughed and drummed his heels like a child. The chuckle, deep in his throat, was moist and thick with tobacco juice.

Elizabeth checked her lipstick in her compact mirror and her teeth for flecks, then wafted a chiffon scarf over her head, tying it in a bow under her chin. Her lilac perfume drifted out of the chiffon and into the dark room like summer rain after a drought.

She sat in the armchair beside Ralph and grasped the steering wheel that hovered in the air in front of the nest of coffee tables. She selected first gear from the magazine rack between the chairs. The new *Radio Times* jutted from the old knitting patterns.

She wished she could sit on the front step and read it from cover to cover with a cup of tea like she did as a newly-wed, waiting for the butcher to strut up the path, his bloody tray clutched against his striped apron. Liver, kidneys or mince, she let him guide her to the best choice.

Once, he left an ox-heart on the step while she was out and she didn't know about the long braising it needed. Ralph couldn't penetrate it with their sharpest knife. He even tried his old army pen-knife, kept greased and primed for any eventuality. But he'd had to make do with crackers and cheese.

"Don't forget the handbrake, dear," Ralph cackled. "And don't lurch. That'll make me feel sick again."

Elizabeth made the noise of the engine. Ralph joined in, louder than his wife and far more excited. He mimicked the change in sound, as she raised her left foot from the tin of sardines serving as the clutch and pressed her right foot on the accelerator of spaghetti-hoops.

It was a miracle, Elizabeth always thought, that she could drive so competently, having never had an opportunity to learn.

"Oh, you've stalled it," Ralph said, clapping his hands on his knees with frustration. "Try again. Give it a bit of choke."

Elizabeth restarted the engine, watching Mrs Causeley pass the window, wrapped in her good camel coat and grappling with Maria, her marmalade wig. She was fearful of these windy mornings, but never missed a Tuesday at Genevieve's on the corner. Genevieve washed, set and teased Maria while Mrs Causeley burrowed into the cocoon of widows' gossip and sweet tea.

Elizabeth used to walk with her. It was the one sparkling segment in her week, but now Mrs Causeley just glanced in as she hurried by, a plastic rain-hat crackling in her pocket to protect Maria should the heavens open on the walk back.

The delivery boy knocked at the door.

"Ignore it," Ralph muttered. He wanted to get started. He had a mountain to climb.

"But it's the groceries, dear."

"Well, leave the engine running and don't dally about."

Elizabeth climbed out, opening and closing the car door as elegantly as she could. Ralph didn't like her to slam it.

"Bang! Oh, Elizabeth, that was rough. You'll ruin this car. Open it again. And close it properly this time."

"But Ralph, I did my best. It's fine."

Ralph crumpled like a scolded toddler and fiddled with the ribbing of his cardigan cuff.

Elizabeth sighed and repeated the motion with a serenity she did not feel.

She yearned for a perm. The ammonia stench from the home kits made Ralph feel ill. Today, the mirror had confirmed that no vestige of her curls remained.

She only ever had sugar in her tea at Genevieve's. It was always in the spoon on every saucer on the tray. Everyone there took sugar, whether they did at home or not. Just as Royal Crown pomade was smoothed into everyone's style, coaxing identical helmets of curls that lasted until the next Tuesday. Once the Royal Crown took effect, they all looked like the Queen. They held their heads higher when they left, saying they hoped the weather held fair until they were home. They hurried in case the heavens opened, anxiously glancing up at any clouds daring to track across their sky.

Elizabeth had tried sugar in her tea at home, but it wasn't the same. And on car days, Ralph wouldn't let them drink anything before they arrived at their destination. He didn't approve of toilet stops.

Thirst cemented her tongue to the roof of her mouth. It was difficult to say 'Good Morning' to the grocery boy with soft skin and a smile that was only for her. Mrs Causeley couldn't possibly be treated to it. She was an old bat, really. Built like a man. Whereas Elizabeth had retained her femininity and her slender ankles. Before she opened the door, she always tugged out the curler lodged in her fringe to entice it to wave.

The grocery boy had a look of her old butcher. It was the fleshiness she noticed. Mallowy cheeks, a solid waistline, meaty arms and a uniform. She loved uniforms, like the butcher's pink-streaked apron and this boy's brown coat flapping about in the wind.

She was a tea-shop waitress in Lyons when she met Ralph. The thrill of sliding into her black dress and knotting the ties of her blinding white apron had never diminished. She could feel it now, like a secret pulse.

One morning, Ralph came into Lyons for a tea-cake and said she was the nippiest nippy there. He came in every day, circling his cap in his hands while he watched her scoot about. After a year of mustering the courage, he asked if she could please stop still for two seconds and agree to go with him to the Alhambra on a Friday night. He was so nervous he had to visit the Alhambra lavatory in the middle of the film to be sick.

Getting married to Ralph ended her career. She settled into Monday washing and Friday polishing and Saturday baking in a pinny run up by Ralph's mum on her old Singer.

It was a long journey to nowhere every day. Ralph called it the trip to anywhere.

"Where are we going today, dear?" he said now.

"Why, to our destination of course, Ralph," Elizabeth replied, as she always did.

He became breathless, grasping her waist with his awkward fingers. He wanted a picnic today. She reminded him of the time, the need to avoid the rush-hour, or the possible queues at the picnic spot if the weather turned fair. Ralph's fervour subsided into fretting. He leapt out to butter bread with frantic haste. He tipped salt for their tomatoes into a scrap of paper that he screwed into a mangled twist. And Elizabeth turned away for a moment to look out of the window at the world hurrying by.

She took the box of food from the boy. Their hands touched. She felt flustered and hot like the spring day forty years ago when the butcher brought his tray into the house. He'd picked up the lambs' hearts and cradled them in his palm.

"I slashed them," he said, "to remove blood clots."

But Elizabeth wanted to stuff them. If she forced the stuffing into an atrium, it would fall out through a ventricle.

He gave her one to hold and she traced the cut with a fingernail.

"No need to be squeamish with fresh meat," he'd said, his young breath eggy and sweet from his breakfast. "Feel that springiness, think how tenderly that will melt in your mouth."

"But the cuts!" she'd said. "My stuffing is all made."

"Ah, now all you need," he said, coming closer and piling the hearts into her hand, caging them with his own, "is a bacon bandage."

He told her how to cross the rashers over the hearts in a star shape and secure them with his butcher's twine. He cut a length ready for her. Ralph would never know what an operation it had been to make his tea. She would be the perfect wife. He would never know how the butcher demonstrated the procedure in the kitchen Ralph had worked overtime to fit for her and how the working of the meat had continued on the dining table Ralph had fashioned from factory off-cuts of medium-density fibreboard. How the flesh pressed deep and frantic into the wood fibres, leaving a pale red stain that would always puzzle Ralph.

Elizabeth put the box of groceries on the kitchen worktop. Ralph was desperate for her to resume position. She paused, remembering how the boy's hands had touched hers. She pressed her palms together, married up her fingertips, feeling the heat transfer one to the other.

"Elizabeth, the starting-handle's fallen off."

She pulled on her gloves. She could catch Mrs Causeley. She could still run. Everything was in perfect order. Firm legs, clear lungs, alcohol-free liver, pink and pumping heart, stout kidneys. She was full of juicy blood, sound organs, healthy tissue. Lots of lean muscle, little fat. She would look appetising hung on a butcher's hook for customers to fight over. They would all want a piece. She was woman. Real woman.

She tugged on her flat boots and mackintosh. Her purse was fat with money she never had a chance to spend on these long journeys with Ralph all day.

"Elizabeth, are you there? My window's stuck, I think. I can't make myself heard."

She tried not to stand on the loose floorboard that always screeched.

"Come on," he called. "I need you, Elizabeth. And you left it in gear, you know! Tch, tch!"

She opened the front door and the sweetest air rushed in. A bus disgorged shoppers and schoolchildren. The street was drenched with the joyful spillage from homes that looked like hers.

Elizabeth wanted to run out there and leap into the huge basket on wheels pulled along by the smart woman in checked trousers, or into the arms of the tattooed man who carried a dog with a plastered leg as fondly as a new-born child. Or under the hissing wheels of the bus.

Into or under anything, as long as it was somewhere out there.

A couple walked by with two children and suitcases. The family were hurrying to the bus station to start a holiday on the coast. Their excitement surged in a wave that engulfed Elizabeth.

She could see a shrimping net clutched in the little boy's hand, see them tasting battered rock-salmon and salt on their lips as they beetled along, smiling at nothing, glancing at the lady in the chiffon headscarf who stared from her front step.

She could have had a grandson of that little boy's age by now. Every passing child became a welcome substitute for what was lost, like a warm current within a cool sea.

She had tasted the salt of change, even though she had never moved away from this street.

She was born across the road. After she and Ralph were married and crammed into the box-room at her mum and dad's, they started saving for this house. It took years to go those few yards.

But when she held their key for the first time, she thought it was the best day of her life. She held hope.

Ralph talked to her all the time of the great adventure their life would be and how the world waited for them out there. But even in the tight-tucked bed, he conserved his own strip of candy-striped territory. Soon his mind ceased to make contact with her too.

Yes, she had tasted salt. It was a hormonal taste, she learned from a book out of the library van that parked in the street on Wednesdays. Pregnancy alters a woman's sense of taste, but it couldn't alter Elizabeth's life any more than that.

She didn't tell the butcher. He knew the ways of flesh too well. She didn't want him to tell her how this scrap of life would be easily detached and disposed of, like the unwanted feathery lungs of a crab being dressed for a special lunch. It would be day-to-day meat work for the butcher. Besides, there was no point. She hadn't seen him round here for a long time. He always said that when he had made his fortune from flesh he would fly away to a flat in Spain and eat roast peppers every day while his toes dipped into his pool.

Under her breath, she wished the passing family a happy holiday. They didn't even see her lips move.

Ralph was revving in his armchair. "The traffic's piling up behind us, Elizabeth. They're all hooting."

She inhaled the essence of the drenched flowers tilting their heads towards the sun. She filled her lungs with it, until they were almost bursting.

Then she took off her outdoor things, shut the front door, quietly as always, and made her way back inside.

BONANZA TULLY'S BABY

Bonanza Tully left her baby by the river the day of the pig roasting. It weren't a good place. Slimy silver gravel. All those sinking holes. The pram, a creaking crate on wagon wheels, was lopsided already and she'd only just walked away from it, striding up the bank in that way she had. One arm crooked, fingers splayed, hips rocking like a pendulum.

I waited for her to turn round. I was hot through, like the sun was spearing my back, but she kept on walking. She was as far as the double oak when I knew she weren't coming back any time soon.

Seems like I spent my entire life waiting to see her, then closing up like a startled clam. Today was different. I decided that at sun-up.

Didn't know if she'd seen me at the shack there. I'd fancied her eyes were on me for a second. But I was kinda tucked into the rotting porch, the broken wood splintering my backside, pondering my new direction. And she'd appeared.

My heart did a hoe-down up against my ribs. Same as always, but with a new twist. Like a floozy in red net skirts wriggling her shoulder at you and winking.

I'd heard a squeak in a regular kinda rhythm. I'd thought mouse. Clamped in the jaws of a feral cat. I wanted to take it in the

147

shack and make a nest with that bit of stiff blanket stuck to the sodden ole boards.

But it was pram wheels I heard. I think Old Man Tully had kinda nailed them on all anyhow. Whisper is that he pilfered two from Josh Napper's buggy and the others from Zuleika's Hardware. Those wheels hollered like piglets on a spit. With each turn the square-dancing floozy cranked up her pace.

The pram had been stuck there a fair time when the early sun broke through the timbers. I felt Clem Coffee's tread flattening the grassy bank behind me. The cattle slowly raised their heads, glistening with dew, curling down their eye-lids against the glare.

"Ya bin with Bonanza?" Clem's breath was hot on my face as he swung hisself in a great arc on the porch strut. I wished it would give way.

I stayed silent.

"She got that swine basted yet, d'ya think?"

"Guess so, Clem. She's done it every July since she turned ten year old."

"Lookin' swell, ain't she?" Clem was eating his Ma's cake, his jaws threshing away like a combine.

We all got this photograph at school. Marking the end. A city man like a mole in a sweating collar came with a tall, hooded camera. I threaded through the huddle to git next to Bonanza. Her hair was like silver rain. And Miss Mather, her lumpy face all screwed up, said yeah, it sure was right enough having the dumbest in the same row.

I rubbed my thumb over Bonanza's grainy face at nights 'til it was nearly worn away. She made me feel ready to start over. Having her in my hands got my courage up and kicking.

Clem kicked at a pile of ants, exploding them into streaks of ragged black goin' every which way, hard at it.

"What's that doin' there?" He flicked his head at the pram and spat out the caraway seeds stored in his mouth.

I stared at the frayed blouse Clem was wearing. It was his big sister's. His Ma turned her girls' stuff into shirts for her one boy. It still had a frill on the edge of the collar. He'd tried to fold it under. And it was goddamn pink.

I willed the strange wheezing from the pram to stop. I could do that. Make things happen, or make things stop. Didn't always work. Didn't stop Old Emmanuel Tully trying to fish naked for dabs from the roof of his barn in the moonlight.

The noise stopped. Clem hurled out a few more seeds. He pulled off his clothes, all set to grapple with the greenish film atop the river. The ducks fussed and started the pram whining again. Clem forced hisself down into the thick depths and disappeared.

I inched my behind a little ways off the porch. Babies round here get ignored mostly, left to grizzle, but this one was in danger of listing into the river. Ten minutes would do it. That could mean I got to see Bonanza again real soon. She would have thrown it right in if she'd wanted it drowned.

Folk here said it had two heads on account of being sired by her daddy. Couldn't believe that. Emmanuel's soaked hisself in Scotch whisky night and day ever since he stopped burrowing out that new tunnel. Saw the minerals in a vision, he said, his beard frothing with spittle. Had a stake in a good mine, but sold it quick, squandered the cash. Then he was after discovering his own little pocket. Like thousands of others camped out in their potato-sack tents, whisky bottle chimneys poking out the top.

"Richer veins," he would roar, strutting through the seamed land, as though he could see clean through the earth to the silver below. "Feel 'em vibratin' in my soul." And off he went scratching the mountain dirt for colour. Buried ore ain't easy to find.

He became superstitious. If a magpie swaggered across his path, he'd grab a gun.

He cursed the sticky blue soil on his pick. Didn't recognise silver ore worth two thousand dollars a ton. A blind man searching, he was. His baby daughter became the only bonanza he would know. And he used her up same ways as he wasted his cash.

Clem surged up and shook like a cur, a thousand rainbow drops flying from his hair. Water sure could look clean that way. Like most other things in this life, depends on what way it finds to present itself.

Clem loomed out onto the mud, paraded a bit, cocky, watching for Bonanza to come back, his skin all raised up in pimples. I willed her to come and give him the hard eye. Wither him.

"Could be mine," he crowed, thrusting his thumb towards the pram. "Ain't seen the thing yet. Sinkin', ain't it?"

The pram was quiet. Higher up in the copse there came a whole lotta strikin' and rustlin'. We turned.

Bonanza was sparking up her fire in a clearing. She were sat facing our way, astride a tin pail with her pale skirts and petticoats all bunched out around her and her slender feet planted on the earth, toes curled in. Her arms were like ribbons, but they worked like a miner's, on and on, sparking that fire, stopping only to set up her spit.

Through the trees the sun shafted onto her as she worked. We heard the echoes a second after she made the movements. Her milk-laden bosoms faltered above her bodice as she rubbed the sticks together. I thought Clem, shining and naked beside me, would burst. Taut and silent, we watched the fire blaze into life.

I saw her look up, skin flushed, a patch of dirt on one cheekbone. Clem slunk behind me and coaxed his trousers up his quivering legs.

I looked at Bonanza and I saw answers. I was gonna take her with me. I was willing it to happen. I'd get myself a job in Virginny City. Maybe in a newspaper office. Smallest ant on the hill. But I wouldn't trek back home at nights. I'd find us a boarding-house. Some were dirt cheap. I could sit at a counter while Bonanza nursed the baby. Leave my beer jar behind me here, just leave it on the sill, walk away from it and be a man instead.

She looked at me again and her purple-black eyes were soft like Ma's stewed damsons. Huge and liquid. They were saying something. Was she telling me to get rid of Clem? He was in a fix with the crotch of his trews, cursing and jumping like a summer bull-frog.

"Clem!"

We both froze. It was his Ma.

I snuck a look up to the track, glimpsed her red plaid shirt, beefy arms crossed over it like a butcher's. He was in for it.

"Done your chores, Clem?" I asked him.

"What the hell d'you think?"

"Clem!" She was louder now. Set the cows lowing and pacing.

"Clem!"

Then there was an echo. Except it wasn't.

"Clem!"

Bonanza was calling, her face distorted by the smoke. I fancied she was smiling in a kinda beckoning way at Clem, but it was just the bleary twisting of air above fire. Made me feel dizzy. Weak.

But she was calling Clem right enough. And his Ma was hollering louder. Bonanza was standing and shouting and smiling. I felt Clem break into a sweat.

Bonanza was playing with him like a kitten with a shrew. He looked shrunken. His teeth were clattering. His Ma called again. There was a slopping sound as the pram slid deeper into the mire.

Clem ran. He rasped past my shoulder and straight to his Ma. I heard her cuff him round the head.

Blouse Boy.

Bonanza was throwing back her head laughing and she called him again, making him look round. He did, even while his Ma was tugging on his blouse sleeve and fair draggin' him homewards to his chores. Bonanza had her back to me then, but I swear she tore her chemise open, mocking him some more. No surprise. Her body had been portioned out so many times 'gainst her will. Far as I knew, it didn't have anything to do with her no more.

I only knew the girl inside the skin. I knew the Bonanza who nursed old folk and cooked for them that couldn't raise a potato. Spoon-fed them too, she did. Young and old. All the dribblers and moaners. She helped with birthing babies. If there were screams in the black of night, Bonanza would run from the bed in the corner of her kitchen.

When she birthed her own kid, she laboured alone, folk said. No one lifted their ass for her.

Bonanza stoked up her fire again and grinned at me. Her hooks and eyes weren't fastened right. I knew she wouldn't tease me like she did Clem, but there was something different today.

I looked hard when she leaned away to pick up her jar of basting grease. She had a battered leather bag there. I could see it through the smoke. It had a yellow ribbon tied in a bow on the handle. Baby stuff, I guessed.

There was buzzin'. Folk coming for their roast. Bringing beer and vegetables, calling to Bonanza about the pig.

"Can't smell nothing, Bonanza! Where's that baby hog?" Zuleika was shrill, her jowls bobbin' like underset jelly. "Remembered the mustard?"

"If that pig's still suckin' on its ma I'll skin ya alive. Spear ya on the spit instead, girl. Got enough lard on ya to baste yerself, ain't ya girl?" Emmanuel was staggering down the bank with his night-cap still on and his bottle broken, jagged at the neck. He wiped the blood from his beard.

Josh Napper's gang, the Fist Boys, were jostling for a place to sit and drink. Josh's Pa was tied in with an ore pocket that was making a mint. Josh had a cooked chicken, a scarlet silk cravat and a basket of whisky. He pushed past Emmanuel and yelled at Bonanza to spike the hog. He didn't look at her, though. No one did.

They were lookin' at the pram.

The sun was blasting through the shack now. Sweat was weeping down my back and springing out on my forehead. Smoke was scalding my throat. I swear I could breathe in Bonanza too. I knew her smell. Her smell was toil and suffering and pain and pride. I could take her away now. Right this minute. She could smell of apricot roses all day and all night.

But I couldn't move. I watched as she stood to grapple with the roasting spit and anchor it over the flames, testing out the ground, checking it was solid. It wasn't. Too boggy here. No base for a heavy piglet to turn on. Wouldn't be the first time she'd lit a second fire in a better place. Keep the first for baking squash. She had her hands on her hips. This was the time. My time to shine. Never will git no other.

I stood up, a bit rickety from last night's ale. I had to hang onto a post.

That was when the wagon wheel croaked into the mud and the damn pram tipped toward the water. Sunlight flashed on the black paint. There was no sound. I took a step. Bonanza didn't move.

"I'm havin' my wheels back!" Josh shouted, showing off to his gang.

"Bonanza Tully, get that stinking crate out the mire and hand over my wheels too!" Zuleika's black frock was strained so tight it was turning grey. She leant on the shack and I felt it quaver.

The town was pouring down like an ant colony on the move. Searching for their hunk of pork, drooling, smacking their lips, waiting for full bellies.

Excepting old Emmanuel Tully, who didn't know sunrise from moonshine. He knew his girl needed crushing, is all. That and his hopeless quest is all he knew.

"Richer veins I'm gittin' me today, boys. Better than your Pa's piss-hole pocket, Josh Napper. Thicker seams. Gittin' myself outa here." He was roaring above the thunder of the fire, above the creaking, above the hard breath of the great wind goading the flames.

It was a rash wind, ours. It quickened up the clouds from the west. It blocked the light. The day turned purple. And a gust rocked the pram right over. Turned it upside down in the river. It started off downstream.

Zuleika screamed like a spanked toddler and the Fist Boys looked around. I sank down kinda heavy. We all stared, shock-fixed on the bloody bundle floating out from the pram and sailing fast away.

"The freakin' pig," Josh said in disbelief. "Bin breathin' its last in the goddam perambulator. Reckon its throat weren't slit all the ways through."

I took another step. Bonanza was looking my way. The shouting started. The fellas jumped in to get the wheels, directed by Zuleika and Josh.

The rain came, nailing us to the spot, Bonanza and I. She picked up the bag with the yellow bow and eased it a bit more open. She held it up to show me a little baby in a white suit, waving its fists at me. She kicked at the drenched fire and it left a dirty plume of smoke between us.

When it cleared, she was already stridin' up the bank in her way, wet dress clinging to her legs, the bag cradled in one arm, the other cocked as usual.

I knew there would be a bus on the main street and I knew sure as hell she'd be catching it. It was her dream to get the hell out of here. Just like it was mine. Only she was doin' it.

"That girl ain't got my coffee ready. I can't walk straight without my coffee. Got myself a long ways to go before nightfall. Git her back, boys. Got my plans and she knows it. Git her back here now! Wait up gal. Wait up!"

Her Pa was grunting out the words. Almost pitiful, it was, but Bonanza was walking. On a mission for her own self. Long paces up to the town with her little baby. A thin sliver of sun peeked back out again, blazing right through her transparent hair.

Folks were picking up the pig. Thinkin' of their bellies. Rollin' their stolen wheels back home through the soaking grass. Fighting over the spit and the fire and the drinks. Fists were flailing around.

I thought of Bonanza's white skin and silver hair that I had never touched and her baby with a face like a lily. She wasn't coming home again, I knew that.

"I'll be shovellin' out dollars," Emmanuel yelled, grabbin' folks' arms, telling 'em about his new silver seam.

They all knew there'd be no bonanza. Just another borrusca. Bust.

But Old Man Tully cackled into his beard, placing his palm over the neck of his bottle to keep out the rain. He saw me for the first time.

"Drink, boy?"

I couldn't move my backside from the shelter of the shack no more. My leg hurt like hell. Needed beer to dull the pain. Lost the other in a cave-in down Yellow Jacket Mine. Just came clean off. I can stand on one leg, but that don't get you far. Cave-ins killed a man a week, so I guess I was lucky.

Today wasn't different no more. I sure hoped Clem would git let out again and bring us some jars of ale. Had to top up. Else I'd start seein' things clear.

Old Man Tully corked up his bottle and tossed it over. The cattle raised their heads as I caught it and then lowered their eyes to the grass.

FOLLOWING CANDACE

On our last day in Linden Avenue, Mother taught me how to make fritters and we finished the bandaging after two weeks of work on it. The home-school authority would nod with approval that our timetable included cookery and first aid. Today's early finish for the funeral was acceptable too, especially in the circumstances.

Mother's breadstick bones were splintering with age and brick by brick workmen were dismantling our avenue. At the far end, we could see the arm of the tower crane beckoning. We had packed most of our belongings. Only the polished jars, some cooking equipment and the tools spread out on the white towel remained.

A small flat was waiting for us. The block shifted in a high wind, people said. I dreamed that, one day, Mother would cup me in her hands like a dove, open the slitty window and release me to some picture-book swoop of hills and glitter-trail rivers.

She closed our curtains two weeks ago. Some mornings, I pushed them aside to see the shining avenue, metallic from the sun or steaming patent leather from the rain. The line of trees rasped and clinked in the autumn wind like old gold pouring into a tomb. All summer long, they had waited like heavy new mothers, teeming with life.

When my father and I weaved between their straight trunks on our last walk, we bestowed upon each tree the name and qualities of a goddess. The nearest to our house was Candace. She led an army of ten thousand rebels against the Roman occupation of Egypt. Ament was the furthest. She lived in a tree on the fringe of a desert and welcomed the dead with bread and water, all the time watching the gates to the underworld. The spells of Nephthys guided them through it.

Nephthys was the protector of the dead and their further adventures through the underworld, like some dark comic-book heroine. Mother had called from a window to remind us to honour her too. No time remained to name a tree after her sister Isis, symbol of rebirth and daylight.

Father was holding my hand, his fingers lighter than a leaf.

"I don't wish to continue," he said. "No further. No more."

During his final night, I watched his face grow smooth, those last words circling in my head like an enchantment. He pressed a piece of paper, a healing prayer perhaps, into my hand when Mother was lighting candles. I hid it in my drawer of useless school socks, to help me in the days ahead.

Soon the trees would fall, their grace sawed to a stump in a heartbeat. Worms were burrowing deep to escape the bulldozers. The school-bell would never echo through the avenue again. The new Saver-Smart would smother the entire area.

The school had been a watchful building. Its red walls grew out of the clay like a camellia would grow, the roots scoring through the soil like a network of white rivers. When Mother was a mute, brown child among cream-faced girls who plucked at the serpent coil of her plaits, Linden School welcomed her.

The school became her temple. It cherished obedient girls. She wanted to stay forever, but the huge and filthy world loomed. Her time was up. When she married, she made my father buy this house so she could still see it and eventually watch me walk there every day.

Now the school had gone and Mother kept me at home. The new school in the city would make me lick the mud from my hockey boots, she told me.

I wanted to taste that living mud. I was afraid of being entombed. Since Father died, time had been wrapping around me like a sheath, tightening its grip every day.

The beds were already dismantled, ready for the move. Most of our belongings were contained in tall crates. Only the necessary equipment remained.

Mother lit our long evenings with candles and at night she curled on the floor by my sleeping-bag.

She vanished and reappeared as the flame cowered, then leapt in the dark. Her sighs disturbed my dreams, leading me through slow seas that deepened into blood-red wombs.

I slithered out of the nylon bag and sat on the sill to watch the reflection of the crane's lights winking in puddles. The night was the temple of Nephthys. Mother often stirred and once I turned to see her finger pointing at me just before the candle stub sank into its own pool.

"Let's begin our cookery lesson," Mother said on that last day. "Then we shall have something special to serve guests after the funeral."

We prepared the utensils, laying them out on a clean tea-towel on the white kitchen surface. We had not packed the largest saucepan. It was one of the essentials. I filled it with water and added scoops of salt. We whisked the batter, taking it in turns. I chopped the onions and a large carrot. Mother didn't like to relinquish control, but Father's death had left her weaker. She hoped to fill me with strength for the tasks required of Nephthys.

"This will nourish you, Safiya. Full of good cholesterol and higher in fat than you would believe!"

I worried about this recipe now. Like most girls of my age, I sought slenderness. My mother was trying to fatten me with fritters.

I picked up the rubber spatula and eased the uncombined flour from the edges of the basin. Mother scissored in chives. I floated a bay-leaf and six peppercorns in the brine. The water rose to the boil.

The saucepan was too heavy for Mother to lift and drain the salty water. She gave me instructions and I obeyed until my arms hung limp. At last we were ready to lift out the cooked brain with a slotted spoon, mixing it with beaten egg to achieve a firm texture. Mother was smiling at me as our spoons wound the egg through the claggy mixture that squelched and wheezed like rubber boots in wet mud. I looked away, trying to breathe only the garden smell of boiled herb and onion.

We rolled the brain in our hands, forming small cakes to dip in the batter and deep-fry until the fritters turned crisp and yellow. Mother held out a finger crowned with a fleck of the mixture.

"Lick this, Safiya," she said, the finger in front of my face.

My instinct was to step back. But my obedient tongue reached out and curled round the speck. The brain slithered in my mouth. It had the texture of silken custard. Mother withdrew her cleaned fingertip and smiled at me.

"Good?" she said.

"Very good. Yes."

At the wake, I would say the fritters were a favourite family recipe. Cheese and onion, perhaps, would ring true.

Mother dressed the table with a blinding white cloth. The folds over the corners looked blue tinged. Nothing could ever be pure white. The hint of another hue always crept in.

"It looks blue, Mother," I said.

She whisked it off the table and pummelled it in the kitchen sink. A goddess must have lent her the strength. She marched it to the launderette on the corner to watch it leap and flail in the hot air of the drier.

I began the first aid class. Unaided. The solitude rolled a

weight off me like August sun fries away morning haze. I could breathe, I could think, I could see.

No one at school had lived like this and I couldn't even exist on the edge of their lives now. The darkness of death cornered me in the house. And the long passage through deeper darkness to eternal life was a journey I believed in no longer.

No more. No further. The words were threaded like beads on an unknotted string. No more of this world, or no more after it? I had no idea.

I tore the white sheets into long strips that shed tiny particles. The sun set the dust motes spinning.

As I worked, I listened to the rumble of the heavy machinery grating the avenue to rubble. I had almost finished one neat toe bandage when Mother came in.

"They were dismantling the fittings while the cloth dried," she said. "I was the only person there. Maybe the last. The manager was writing a sign. *Thank you to our loyal customers.*"

Mother sank into a chair. We listened to the lorries, to the whine of the crane's swinging arm, to the clack of the kitchen-clock.

"Let us move fast," Mother said. "Another layer of bandages, Safiya. The next toe, please."

Father still smelt clean from the washing, the rinsing in wine and the massage of sweet oil. The rich smell of palm still pervaded the house.

Since bacteria can still thrive after the passing of their host, my deft palms and Mother's slow fingertips had oiled him after death, hers shaking, as they anointed each dear crease or traced a well-loved line within his skin. Sometimes her finger pressed the oil onto her own lips, then along his papery cheek.

The sterilised tools lay in a row on a white towel and we cut his left side with care, removing each organ with grace and precision for storing in the jars with animal heads for lids. He had fired them all at the Technical College's Wednesday evening pottery classes. But he was too ill to glaze them. So Mother and I brushed on the sheen for him, while he gave us his gentle smile.

Soon after death, Mother had inserted a long thin hook through his nostril to break up his brain, enabling us to coax it down and out of his nose. It took time, but we were patient, removing every piece with care and placing it all in a good freezer-bag.

The bandaging took time, because we wrapped his head, neck, fingers and toes as separate entities, then encased the limbs several times over. He was a small man, but we took care to make the mummification perfect.

Today, we bound the arms and legs together, placing a scroll inscribed with words from the *Book of the Dead* between his cottony hands, which felt sturdier now from the layers of bandage. The spells would ward off evil spirits that might otherwise hinder his journey through the underworld.

"He is preserved and sanitised to perfection," Mother announced as we went to the kitchen to check the frying-pan. She seemed stronger now, younger, as if the fresh white linen and gleaming oils had purified her own soul. "Safiya, you and I are protected from anguish. His good heart is travelling towards the clear light of eternity."

In the garden, I had already dug a hole where a bank of lilies had finished blooming. Saver-Smart would not need to churn the earth there for their foundations. We had scrutinised the plans. Our little piece of territory would form part of the planted area required by the planning authority to provide greenery, together with a slatted bench and stone litter-bin with cigarette-stubber. The supermarket would rise in a matter of weeks once the whole of Linden Avenue was removed.

Mother and Father had decided his death-chamber should be somewhere sacred, somewhere no one could disturb again. There was no point coring out a segment of beautiful land that would be

161

sacrificed one day, dragging out his pure soul and interrupting its quest.

"Safiya, the guests will arrive soon. They'll help us carry Father. The manager of Saver-Smart is going to say a few words at the graveside. Gather the jars, will you, dear?"

I caressed the jackal-head lid of the jar containing his stomach. I kissed Hapi, the baboon-head that housed his lungs. The cancer had intruded there first.

Mother placed a hand on my shoulder. "Safiya, remember, please, I have explained to you about Nephthys, the goddess of the mortuary. She protects Hapi, helps him to guard Father's ailing lungs."

No more words were needed. She turned to flip the fritters with her fish-slice. She rested each one on absorbent paper. I arranged them on a platter in the middle of the table.

I looked through the window at the workmen holding back the tape barrier for guests to pick their way through the rubble of Linden Avenue. I recognised the Saver-Smart manager. Mother had promised to keep the occasion very private, just trusted friends, so that future customers would not 'get spooked' as he had first suggested might be the case. The garden was still our land, at least for a little longer. He respected that. He was a former pupil of Linden School. He knew how monstrous life outside could be.

As soon as I saw him catch my eye, I knew I would soon be wearing the red-striped uniform and stacking the Saver-Smart shelves with jars and bottles in the section overlooking the patch of green.

Mother called me. The food was ready and my dear father was waiting. The guests were arriving. I'd never be able to leave now.

I stayed at the window a moment longer. Candace, the leader of the rebel army and the next in line to fall, was swaying. Her branches stretched like arms towards me, as if in some prosaic prayer. Her leaves stirred, the familiar flimsy rustle of old gold. In my pocket, Father's piece of paper was whispering to me.

I had looked at it this morning. It showed a bank account number and my name. It told me to keep my feet on the ground and I laughed like any schoolgirl at the irony that this pass to the future had been nestling in my sock drawer.

I remembered more of my lessons about Nephthys. That she was also goddess of the air, she was a wild bird created by air and she was the source of rain and the River Nile.

Her sister Isis was the symbol of dawn, birth and growth. Nephthys depicted night, death and decay. But one was not the reverse of the other, my father had told me. They were different reflections of the same reality, all of them bound with life.

I opened the door to the mourners and walked past them all. I told them about the fritters so they could be clear about the contents and make their own choice whether to eat them. And I ran along Linden Avenue in the sun, until I was one heart bursting.

Opening Time

Ian Green unlocked the door of his bed shop to the cotton and plastic odour of his shrink-wrapped mattresses and linen. The same smell every day for twenty years. He had never given it a thought before.

The same early morning people went by, keys clattering, releasing the shutters of their own shops. Was his face pinched, his eyes tightened like theirs? Would they listen in vain, like Ian, for the cling of the till, while the rest of the world clicked keys at home?

As retailers rushed to their positions, Ian always saw a lone man take a route to his allotment through the Parade, a hoe hoisted over one shoulder and a bag of compost in his other hand. Today, Ian wasn't sure if this man with his chipped black fingernails and mulch-stained boots was real.

Ian could feel the wind in his hair despite being inside. He smelt earth and heard birdsong. There were no trees in the Parade. Only bins and a bench with a missing plank. But within his shop, Ian felt the air and the sounds from outside, as the allotment man, face tilted to the sun, strolled by.

Belinda and Ruth depended on Ian. They lived and planned and shopped, while he unlocked this door and stood at his counter, smiling at anyone who passed by, calculating whether he would make enough profit for this month's mortgage and next summer's holiday.

This morning Belinda had asked for a cheque for Ruth's school trip to Alaska. Hundreds of pounds. Ruth had glared when he hesitated, the letter fluttering in his hand.

He put his flask of lentil soup on the draining board in the back room. His father had always closed the shop for lunch. But Ian couldn't afford to miss a sale. Few enough people bought beds and bedding from his shop these days. The odd customer buzzed around the divans, asked if he stocked antique-effect brass or cheap French lace eiderdowns, which he didn't, and then stung him with a look of disbelief.

Ian plugged in the kettle. Glanced at the clock. Ten minutes before opening. Time to make tea and hide it beneath the counter among his carrier bags and spare till-rolls. It wouldn't do for customers to see him sipping as if he were only half-available. He had visited shops where assistants leant against walls or chewed gum. He would never present anything other than alertness, a veneer of dedication to duty.

But this morning Ian felt different, drained of himself. His body performed all the professional shopkeeper actions, but the moment he had signed that cheque for Alaska, his soul slipped like raw egg white down a plughole.

Ruth had stuffed the cheque in her shiny schoolbag and discussed the list of essential clothes with Belinda. They'd giggled at the prospect of thermal longjohns, realising that dreary fundamentals could, in fact, be lace-trimmed and sensual.

Ruth was just thirteen, but she and her mother had formed an alliance. Ian hovered on the edge, while they coveted new things and incinerated all that was out of fashion.

Ian placed his mug on a tin lid from a tub of paper clips, his coaster for twenty years. He checked his watch. A minute left.

He didn't fancy his tea today. A film gathered on it while he stared at the mattress waiting for Miss Dangerfield. He had dreamt about her last night. He didn't usually dream. Belinda and Ruth discussed the symbolism of their dreams over breakfast, embellishing half-remembered fragments to concoct a credible story, disassembling the dreams to make sense of them.

"I was chased by a wolf into a cottage in the woods. And a girl with long red hair made me eat a whole apple pie and then throw the empty plate on the fire. What on earth did it mean, do you think, Ruth?"

"Well, remember we saw that nature programme and there were wolves on that. Then you were looking at the properties page in the paper and you said how much you fancied a weekend retreat in the country. Then I told you that Millie Locke at school had dyed her hair and it came out burgundy and she hated it. And we said we should get new china now our set's been discontinued. Apart from the apple-pie, which I'd have to think about, it's all there, Mum, when you really look at it."

She had stitched these scattered elements together, in control of every moment, even the unbidden fantasy hours of the night.

Ian's dream with Miss Dangerfield had risen from nowhere; wild, vivid, savage. Like a scene from a film, it replayed in his mind. Their flesh suctioning together, beautiful with sweat, raw and glistening like the first ooze of juice from roasting meat, raised and beaded on Miss Dangerfield's brown breasts and thighs.

Ian's dream was pure passion. Nothing hidden. Yet he could not reveal it at the breakfast table. Couldn't let the details be picked over like the bones of the Sunday chicken.

Until this morning, he hadn't known his world was clouded with the dust of routine and expectations. He performed rituals every day to keep the roof over his family's head. Ordering, stacking, banking, accounting, changing till rolls, plumping up pillows on display beds. Retailing ran through his veins and fed his heart.

But his heart had never pumped like it did when Miss Dangerfield first came into the shop to enquire about affordable foam-filled versus pocket-sprung.

He felt hot when he thought about her hired van drawing up. She had many things to collect today from all sorts of places. An antique bed warmer from the junk shop, a broken grandfather clock from a friend's late father's house and a box of ramshackle garden tools she'd won at auction. She hadn't found the courage to bid until the last lot was called, but the assortment in the box fascinated her, she'd told Ian. Wind-chimes, terracotta pots, an ancient trug, a scythe.

Ian usually made polite, but detached, conversation with customers.

"A scythe indeed. How splendid," he would have said to anyone else.

But he had wanted to keep Miss Dangerfield in his shop. Store her. Watch her all day. Lock her in all night.

"You must be careful with a tool like that, Miss Dangerfield. Incredibly hazardous, those sorts of blades. I could give you a hand. I used a scythe as a lad on my uncle's farm."

Ian's uncle had asked him to live at the farm and work the land the day after Ian's father handed him the keys to the shop. Ian had looked down at his fingernails, crusted with his uncle's red soil, and slowly shaken his head, the shop key heavy in his trouser pocket, pressing against his thigh.

"Do you have a large garden to tame?" he asked Miss Dangerfield.

And she had laughed and said it would just be ornamental, the scythe. She would mount it on a stone wall and enjoy its elderly rust spots and worn handle.

His father had trained him to keep a respectful distance, not over-involve himself. Otherwise, customers would come in any old time just to chat. And that was totally unprofessional. The butcher was overbearingly amiable. He had women leaning against his counter making sheep's eyes at him when he should have been chopping and boning, Ian's father always said. It looked bad, the boundary between retailer and consumer being smudged like that. Same as marriage. There had to be respect for each other, a degree of separation.

Ian wanted to climb inside Miss Dangerfield.

He had never seen his parents embrace, never imagined them having sensations beneath their sturdy, practical clothes. It made him hot and uncomfortable to think about it. His father even wore a tie when he cut the grass on Sundays. When they grew old, they sat in blankets in their beach hut, his father saying how retirement gave them the proper, endless holiday a shopkeeper could never take during his working life. Yards away, the sea murmured, bitterns boomed in the marshes and children squealed on the beaches. But, by then, Ian's parents were too deaf and weary to hear.

Ian checked the time in a mechanical way, as if he were wound up and set to do so, as if he were a clock himself.

And for the first time in twenty years, he was late opening the shop. His father, were he still alive, would be appalled.

But Ian stayed where he was, watching the second hand labour full circle. During that minute, in contrast to the clock's refusal to alter its unbroken tempo, his heart throbbed faster.

Blood flooded his jowls, diffused in spider-leg fashion over his cheek-bones. He felt as if he were steaming. Perspiration crawled between his shoulder blades.

Tyres rasped on the sodden road. A handbrake rattled. He wanted to look, but savoured the anticipation. It sent every hair on his body upright in slow motion.

She had actually gripped his arm and giggled about the thrill of hiring a van for the first time in her life. The cottage, inherited from her grandmother, was almost derelict, but she could hardly wait to camp out under the sagging ceilings. The staircase had rotted away. She would haul the mattress into the kitchen where the floor was almost in one piece. Then she patted his arm before releasing her grip.

No one had grasped him like that before, with warmth that fired through his veins. He felt it now, watching her jump down from the driver's seat.

She looked confused by the 'closed' sign. Ian's legs sprang into motion.

"I'm so sorry, Miss Dangerfield. Can't think why the shop's not open yet."

He spoke as if the shop were shirking responsibility. As if the premises had nothing to do with Ian Green, proprietor of Green's Bedding for twenty years.

Miss Dangerfield ran her hands over the shrink-wrapped mattress. Ian watched the polythene ripple under her fingers.

"Would you like a cup of tea before we load it?"

"Oh, that's kind of you, Mr Green, but I do have to make my rounds and collect all my motley objects. In fact, this mattress is the only sensible investment I've made."

She laughed in that way she had, head tossed back, her generous teeth glittering under the ceiling light.

Ian wished she hadn't bought her one prudent purchase in his shop. He wished he could sell her a tiara or an Alsatian or a blunderbuss.

He stopped thinking. His father, normally imprinted on Ian's soul, slithered away. Ian encased Belinda and Ruth in a block of ice and sailed it across the ocean to the frozen wastes of Alaska.

"Miss Dangerfield, I'm taking the step of actually shutting the shop for the morning. Therefore, I would be happy to assist you. You can't possibly do all that fetching and carrying on your own." His tone was almost belligerent, defying every rule of good retailing code he had been trained to respect.

He wasn't at all sure he felt himself. Yet he had never felt surer. He looked at her young shape in jeans and green jumper, her long russet hair tied in a ponytail, her newness in the bedding shop which had bred him years before her birth.

Miss Dangerfield stepped back. He noticed her eyes were the colour of ripe pear.

"Mr Green, you can't leave your shop to help me. I'm fine, really. I've got help anyway, thank you."

He had stepped over a line. He could feel it, as if a boundary had been chalked in red on the shop floor.

Ian Green had never overstepped before. Ice slid down his back. He looked at the clock, but didn't register the time, just the disapproving droop of the minute hand.

His customer was shrinking away, pushing the mattress out the door to a young man leaping from the van's passenger seat.

They drove away.

Ian left the 'closed' sign on the door, pulled down the shutters, switched off the lights and locked himself in. No one passed the window while he stood there, listening to the fluorescent tubes clicking and flickering as they faded. And if anyone had gone by, they would not have noticed him in the gloom, shadowed by a tower of goose-feather bolsters.

No one tapped on the door to enquire about prices, check opening times, or find out if Ian Green, proprietor for twenty years, still breathed. His dream was beginning to burn his day to ashes.

He would have caressed Miss Dangerfield in the hot van, primed her body for the cool flagstone floor of her cottage and laid down with her on the new mattress, a sturdy purchase with a traditional striped ticking fabric and nice lively springing. Her green jumper reminded him of the sea in summer. He imagined her naked to the waist, caked in damp sand, her mermaid's tail floundering and soaked, heavy with seawater. He would have carried his mermaid to the mattress and let it absorb the sea from her drenched skin. He would have licked the sand from her face, his tongue clearing it in long swathes that filled his mouth with warm gritty ocean. They would have dragged the mattress out into the sun afterwards and watched it dry, a good test of the droplet-resistant material.

But all his passion hung in the air. Just a wisp of smoke merging with the air after a bonfire has finally died.

No one needed Ian Green. Belinda and Ruth would write their own cheques with the life insurance fortune he would leave them.

"Protect your stock. Protect your premises. Protect your family," his father had always said.

And so Ian Green was vigilant with security locks and alarms. He was precise with premium payments. Rock solid. Belt and braces. Watertight.

But the shop was on the slide. No one wanted to pay the italic prices he wrote on his cardboard swing tickets.

The allotment man had never come into Green's Bedding. And he didn't look like a man who tapped on a keyboard at home. He looked like a man who dreamt uncomplicated dreams and pulled cabbages and onions from the earth to carry home for his family to cook.

Ian would slide with his shop. His passion was spent like a match lit in a gale.

He went to the kitchen at the back and unscrewed the top of his thermos. He poured the lentil soup into the sink and watched it drain. He drank a glass of tap water from the tumbler he had kept on the ledge for all of the twenty years.

He thought about his uncle's farm and how he had fed and watered the animals and the soil. How they sucked and snaffled and snatched without hesitation or gratitude.

He picked up the matches beside the gas ring his father had used. Ian didn't bother with it. He had treated himself to the electric kettle. His father would have enjoyed flicking it on, hearing

171

the water surge and listening for the clunk of the switch telling him his water was boiled, subsiding now, the wait over.

Ian Green struck the first match, relieved so many remained. He kept a well-stocked shop. He owned every mattress range the customer could ever need.

He threw the first match onto Comfee Dreemz, the second onto Velvet Slumbers. The third he applied to Cosy Dozy Nights and the fourth blazed well as soon as it touched Snug 'n Sound.

The fire raged. Ian Green felt the spreading heat, but kept his tie knotted and his jacket on.

He went to the far end of the shop with the last match and laid down on the finest mattress from the Destiny range, which he had displayed on a single pine bed from the Deep Peace collection. It was twenty percent off this week.

Naturally, he had remembered to remove his shoes first, as directed by the polite notice to customers trying out his merchandise.

And he eased his mind into the dream-swell of cool sea, letting it lap at first, and finally engulf him.

Ten O'clock to Balham

Alison watched the guard pacing on the cold platform. Through the glass door's frosted ridges, he looked sawn up into shifting, vertical sections. There was something comforting about his strutting gait, the flashes of blue uniform, the occasional shouts of greeting to regular passengers. He had promised to tell Alison when her train arrived.

"No sense hanging abart out 'ere, love. It's not due yet," he'd said, his words kind in the sandpaper wind. "You sit yourself down in the waiting room. It's just for ladies, look. Nice for the babe to be in the warm. I'll give you a shout."

Alison wore a ring. Just a plain gold-coloured band, just like a curtain ring. Her parents had bought it from a catalogue.

"Gives a better impression," they'd told her when she'd left this morning.

But Alison didn't think the guard had looked at her finger. His eyes had met hers, glancing away to the track now and again through shyness, or the need to check points and signals, or whatever guards did.

As he closed the door, Alison felt the baby squirm, working up to overwhelming hunger. It might be less embarrassing to feed him here than on the train. She was quite alone at the moment.

She had just begun, when a woman appeared in the waiting

room, setting her basket on the table. She sat opposite Alison to watch, her head with its dandelion-clock hair tilted to one side. She didn't unfold a newspaper or examine her nails. She just beamed, buttery teeth prominent, pebbly eyes watching.

Alison glanced at the woman's black cape, then up at her mottled face. It reminded her of the pink continental sausage her parents sliced onto a platter for dinner-parties. She smiled back and looked down again at the frantic mouth of her child. He pulled hard, as though this would be his last feed on earth. Alison curved her back into the plastic chair in the dreary room. The electric fire kept clicking. The baby kept sucking. The woman continued to watch and smile.

★

Alison's parents had said, "Call us Pamela and Derek. We're too young to be grandparents. Even 'Mum' and 'Dad' makes us feel old now."

Their estate was full of thrusting nineteen-seventies' couples, their second and third bedrooms filled with Twister sets, demijohns fermenting elderflower wine and Mediterranean holiday brochures.

They moved her into the back bedroom. They bought a record player and a lava lamp to encourage her to stay in. Derek carved the baby's initials into the cot. He used to whittle at weekends, before men all took up squash. When Alison settled on the couch at feeding times, Derek always left the room.

"Oh, can't you go out the back door with the pram?" Pamela said, when Alison pushed it off the front step. "No need to flaunt it to the cul-de-sac."

"I'm not flaunting. Just proud."

"But we have to *live* here, Alison. With all the whispering. Let's be discreet, shall we?"

"Why bother? They must have already seen me looking

enormous. What does it matter anyway? Don't you love your grandchild?"

"Of course! That's what I'm thinking of. We don't want them pointing and staring, do we?"

Alison reversed the pram. It felt like being six and told to face the corner.

When she left this morning, Amanda knew their cloak of parental concern was a shroud for their glee at being Pamela and Derek again.

They offered her a lift. But the main line rumbled behind the tall beeches at the end of the back garden. Alison felt the throb of it through the wall of her bedroom. It pledged her release, thumped out a message, a promise of acceptance from the outside world.

They slid on the ring. It spun round, too large. She had to clamp her fingers together to keep it in place.

★

Now she was baring her shame. Inviting the world to validate it. Turn it into a celebration instead of a cheerless secret. The world was waiting for her. Or at least Balham was.

She straightened her back and listened to the next announcement. She had a few minutes to unhook the baby and transfer him to the other side.

"It's good that you don't feel embarrassed. I do so admire you, you know. No need to hide in the Ladies when baby needs a feed, is there?"

Dandelion leaned on the table, peering closer. Alison sweated and inched her chair back. An express shot through. The woman's basket reverberated on the table.

She peeled off her cape. Underneath she was stout and starched in her nurse's uniform, dominating the room in her royal blue and white.

Alison softened her shoulders and smiled again.

"How long before your train, dear?" The woman tightened her thick elastic belt. The ornate buckle glinted in the fluorescent light.

"Only a few minutes, unfortunately. He's so hungry he'll cry if I stop."

"Got a good set of lungs, has he?" Her grin was close. Alison could smell Trebor mints and feel cold menthol breath on her chest.

"Oh yes."

They listened to the baby's gulping and swallowing, the popping electric fire.

"Does he take a bottle?"

"No. Well, I haven't tried yet. But I really have to. I've got a job in Balham."

It was a relief to say it out loud. Expressing milk had been a tense battle. An hour of pumping had produced a teaspoonful.

"I've got all the stuff, but I'm scared of making the break. You know, whether he'll be deprived of me..." She looked down at her pale-blue bag, engorged with teats and tubs.

The woman rustled over to Alison's side of the table, blocking the light from the door.

"May I?" she asked.

She gathered the equipment and assembled a bottle on the table.

"Unplug him, dear, while I get them to warm this in the café."

Alison sighed as she detached the baby. At least she would be free of these awful wet circles on her blouse. She could hand him and his blue bag over to the crèche in Balham.

She laid the baby on the table by the woman's basket while she dressed. His face flushed red. He drew up his legs. She waited for the screams as she buttoned her blouse and laid him back on her lap.

176

In the pause before the crying began, she felt the growing warmth of his head on her thighs. His curly fingers clenched. Alison felt sick. She pictured him in the crèche, his tiny lips rooting for her, longing for his mother's scent, her voice, her arms. And she would be trapped in a typing pool, lipstick on, lumpy chest still inflating, counting the hours until his head was tucked in the crook of her arm again. Would he know her?

The train rushed into the station as he wailed. She picked him up and laid his furious face against her neck as if he was yelling into her soul.

The guard opened the door as the train rumbled to a standstill. "Ain't this your train, love? Wanna hand?" His hair flopped onto his red face and his trousers were too short for his legs.

Tears were tugging at the backs of her eyes. She had promised herself she wouldn't break down. She buried her face in the baby's cardigan, inhaling the back-garden air trapped in the wool.

"All right love, are you?"

She would have given anything to say, "No. I'm scared. Scared my parents will have already changed the locks. Do you know, Mr Guard, when some old friends turned up for bridge, Pamela and Derek made me pretend my child belonged to a neighbour who had been called away urgently and left us 'literally holding the baby'. They laughed like drains at their wit. Derek barricaded me in the kitchen when I had to do the evening feed. The old friends wanted to see the new fitments with the wood-effect drawer-fronts. But Derek barred their way. They were quite insistent. He stood in the doorway brandishing the soda syphon. It was quite threatening. They left soon after. Even before Pamela had finished threading the cheese and pineapple onto the cocktail sticks"

Alison wanted to explain all this. But she was sure the guard would never understand. He was looking at her child as if he were made of pure gold.

The dandelion hair appeared by the guard's shoulder. "She will be all right, won't you dear? I'll see to that."

The guard looked relieved. "I'll leave her in your capable hands then, Nurse. But she's not got long." He closed the door, adding, "Better keep the heat in, love. Babies feel that chill old wind, y'know."

But Alison could still feel the bitter cold, even though a patch on her right leg was scorched by the tube of electric fire.

The woman crouched, her eyes at the same level as the baby.

"I'll take him, dear. If a stranger does the first bottle, it's easier. If he smells Mum, he'll only want you." She screwed up her mouth, as if the thought left a nasty taste.

Alison held on to the baby. A whistle screeched. Train doors slammed.

The woman's thumbnails picked at her gilt buckle. "Hundreds of mothers have passed their babies to me, dear. Trusted me. I know we've never met, but I love all babies. Lost three of my own, you see. All born blue."

She smoothed her pinafore and held out her arms.

Alison let the woman prise the baby off her soaking neck. In seconds, he was rasping against the starchy royal-blue and white, his mouth full of rubber teat and the room filled with new sucking sounds.

Alison heard a longer whistle and saw the cut-up strips of the gangling guard in the glass panel. "I have to go now," she said.

"You sort out your bags then, dear, and get them on the train. I'll follow with the baby."

Alison picked up her holdall. She would miss the train if she didn't hurry.

"Leave the baby's bag," Dandelion said. "I can manage that."

It was a command.

Alison moved to the door. She had to let others take over now. She'd told herself that. She put her hand on the door handle, then stopped. The guard would help her get on the train. She didn't need the woman now.

But she couldn't be rude. The poor thing had lost her own. Let her have one last minute. After all, Alison's new life wouldn't begin in Balham. It had begun when she left home through the front door. She was in it now.

She turned back and saw the woman's basket on the table. It was empty, apart from a soft blanket printed with orange ducks, the corner turned back.

"All aboard!"

The guard opened the door an inch and called through. "It's off any second, love. Are you going or not?"

He bounded back to the platform, leaving the door ajar.

Alison hesitated. Took one step. She imagined her baby lying in that basket. Covered with the orange ducks. And she thought about being free and flat-chested again in Balham. And sleeping all night long. She took another step.

The guard dashed past. She saw him in the inch-wide gap, then through the glass he was darting along again, panicking about the time. She stood still, the sound of her child's breathing stifled by the train's engine.

"Come on, New Mum! Still going to Balham?"

She could see the guard properly now. He paused to give her a beckoning wave before cupping his long awkward fingers under an old lady's elbow to help her up the step and into her carriage. Like a shepherd with his flock.

He came back for the last time. She could see every spot on his chin.

"New Mum, Balham train's going!"

"Yes, I'm coming. Can you give me a hand please?"

Alison turned back to take her child.

"Thought that old girl was with you," he said on the platform, his red wrists poking out from his cuffs as he took her bags.

"No, I don't know her at all."

"My mum's a nurse too. But they told her to give up wearing that big buckle thing. Carried germs, you see. Haven't worn them for years now. They have quite a modern sort of uniform these days. Drip-dry and that."

Alison looked back. The nurse had vanished.

"Well, here's a nice empty carriage, love."

He let her settle with the baby while he stowed her bags under the seat.

"There you go, my love. Blimey, it's brass monkeys today." He tucked in the trailing ends of the baby's shawl. "I hope you've got a warm home to go to."

He gave her a wink and closed the door.

Through the grimy window Amanda could read his lips.

"Make sure you get someone in Balham to help you get off!"

She smiled and nodded, shifted the weight of the baby until they both sat in comfort. An elderly lady clucked at him, unable to resist smiling at his newness, his innocence, his purity.

Alison realised she was clenching her fingers to keep the ring on. She let it slide off into her bag. The old lady kept smiling and clucking. She didn't need Alison at all. Conversation was unnecessary.

The engine was straining, desperate to begin. Alison clutched her baby, relieved to feel its pressure against her breast, already tensing with new milk in response. The brakes were released. And with an impatient hiss, as if it had held a great breath while it waited, the train moved off. How close she'd come to missing it.

BEFORE THE BIRDS SING

The alarm nudged Mei-Li awake, murmuring in her ear, as if complicit in her plan. She switched it off. But she could still hear it ringing in her head. She had slept with the anticipation and now it was all she could hear.

Cheng remained asleep. Mei-Li peered at the clock-face. Nearly dawn. Easing out of bed, her little bones creaked. The iron bedstead protested, accustomed to serenity. The ringing in Mei-Li's ears faded, replaced by a rush of roaring blood.

She picked up her pills. She should have shaken one free last night. As the tiny capsules shifted in their pot, they became a bottled stampede of clattering hooves in that hushed, empty time before the birds began to sing.

She dressed on the landing and left the house, the city air cool on her face and harsh on her joints. Along the hushed avenues, beneath the hiss of stirring leaves, she was a small blur gliding past the closed eyes of her neighbourhood; a simple dot mingled with the fragments floating within their eyelids as they dreamed.

She passed the parade of shops in the shadow of the skyscrapers beyond. Their glass fronts were shuttered. Litter prowled. Mei-Li heard it compete with the spring wind, felt it whip her ankles. She hurried past the bins, alive with rats foraging before sunrise.

Mei-Li's knees buckled under the weight of age. The pain was raw, but the first haphazard lights glowing in patterns from distant buildings drove her on.

The warehouse was on the edge of the aromatic colours and savoury tangs of the rich inner quarters.

She dismissed the unbidden vision of Cheng, how his body rose and fell, wheezing like a dilapidated accordion in their bed. How his needs had gradually fallen out of kilter with hers. How the prawns she bathed in batter for him jumped back up to contest his digestion, when once he would have let her feed them to him, one by one, pinched between two fingers. No, this moment was hers.

She was close to the warehouse. Two other elderly ladies and a trio of men waited, hunched in wheelchairs. The group gathered in a dignified snaking line, turning to bow in greeting as others joined. Two young girls with withered legs and a creamy-eyed man with a stick completed the assembly.

The great metal doors shifted and every head shot up. The sun seeped rivers of light through the scrubby bushes. The grit of the forecourt vibrated with the faraway rumble of early trams and traffic. The iron doors boomed open.

Out it crept. Silently, solemnly breaking free from its storeroom, green, gold, scarlet and silver. There was not a flicker from the gathering as it bared its teeth like a row of white bunting in its cavernous, crimson mouth, nostrils to the ground. It swung its colossal head from side to side, still close to the dirt, then flung it up, wide-stretched jaws directed at Mei-Li.

The men in chairs leaned forward. Mei-Li forgot her sore, grating bones and stretched up on her toes, clasping her hands.

Trapped for months, a softened heap in a cobwebbed corner, the great Chinese dragon flared from the doorway and into the morning. Eyes of a rabbit, ears of a bull, horns of a stag, claws of a tiger, scales of a fish and the long writhing body of a serpent.

The knot of withered people untangled. They didn't see the human limbs in shining gold track-suits giving life to the great dragon. They saw only his flamboyance, felt him toss their own dreary existences into a sack for safekeeping. They joined the parade.

The dragon, exuberant in the new sun, was a beacon of hope and good fortune. The drum thumped out the beat of the dance.

The great dragon dipped and coiled into a cloud-cave, into a whirlpool, always to the beat of the drum. His dancing legs collaborated, the head workers cooperating with the body movers, the tail team in time with the head. Unity at its purest. Harmony so fine that Mei-Li shook with joy.

She could fly through the morning haze of sunlit exhaust fumes. She could swim through the olive waters of the canal. The drum throbbed in her head, chasing evil spirits away

Some of the golden workers stood on the legs of others to raise the great beast higher. Mei-Li danced alongside, pushing a wheelchair, one of the girls sitting on the lap of its occupant.

An hour passed. Dreams came alive.

But the dragon twisted, writhing around to begin the journey back to its lair. Mei-Li swivelled the wheelchair and hurried alongside, reluctant to miss a moment.

She could feel its fire scorching into her soul, warming from within, giving strength to her hands, power to her legs and might to her heart.

The performance finished at the gaping entrance to the warehouse, its doors still flung wide to readmit its glorious occupant until New Year came round. Today's swift practise, a small treat for those who dream of hope, ended without ceremony. In full view of the audience, the dragon crumpled to the ground and shrank back into the darkness.

The heavy doors closed, hands were shaken, thanks given. Mei-Li and the others exchanged smiles that burned from brown eyes.

The new day began. Factory doors screamed open. The sun glared at them all as they dispersed, turning their backs on the lair until next year.

Mei-Li went home to tidy her spilt pills. A dry bush rustled as she passed. She paused. A rose-finch lifted its carmine head to watch her as it burst into song.

HALF PRICE MONDAYS WITH HÉLÈNE

Jane stepped into Hélène's and began to fade. Half-Price Mondays usually coloured her in like a magic-painting book. Just add water. Or, in Hélène's case, setting lotion.

But Jane dismissed the peculiar feeling in her arm. If she mentioned it, Bunty Roland would make a diagnosis from her *Readers' Digest* medical book. The treatment would encourage a moustache and bloating at the least.

Sometimes, she thought, as Hélène tucked her into the greying nylon cape, it was best to keep niggles quiet. Nothing should interfere with Mondays.

Hélène moved with customary grace in her soft pumps. The swish of her skirt sent the snippings skating across the floor. Damp-cut hair, white and wiry, became fairy-like as it fell and dried at their feet.

Bunty and Kath arrived together.

"Excuse my bottom," wheezed Bunty. "Not being funny, but I don't feel I have to get trussed up for you ladies."

Jane knew the struggle Bunty had with girdles. She heard about it every Monday.

"It's like trying to keep a blancmange in a string bag," Bunty said. "Can't wait to get home and snap my poppers."

Hélène brought Kath the ashtray and transferred Jane to the basin, slotting the back of her neck into the dip. As Hélène coaxed the water to a comfortable warmth, Jane's heart capered. From Tuesday to Sunday she missed being touched.

Hélène's fingertips circled her head, working the shampoo into whipped cream, soothing every contour of Jane's scalp. She could have cried out with relief as the week's frozen solitude thawed.

Bunty and Kath talked above the radio.

"I told him, it's *Smash* or nothing. I'm not scraping potatoes after a late turn."

"Well, teenage boys are supposed to eat anything, duck."

The rinsing water rained down. Jane leaned her head back against the light finger pressure. It was gentler now, tracing her scalp, cupping her ears. She held her breath.

"I know he's my grandson, Kath, but I'm not having language like that in my lounge."

"What did he say, Bunt?"

Jane listened to the gelatinous gulp of the conditioner leaving the bottle. The honeysuckle lotion coated each curl. The slow, deep kneading began.

Please don't forget the nape, she thought, basking in the safe knowledge it was never neglected. Her neck yielded to the extravagant motion. She knew by heart the pathways Hélène would groove with three fingers and the added weight she would apply with her rotating thumbs.

"Well, not being funny Kath, but teenage boys smell like beef."

"They can use those sprays, can't they? I've seen them on television."

"They're for young girls' armpits, Kath. Coal tar's what he needs. Seen Barb, by the way? She's got those screw-in teeth."

"Can she eat?"

"Only Black Forest gateau."

Jane was shepherded back to her first chair. The trainee brought her a cup of tea.

But Jane's arm wasn't working. She couldn't take the tea. The other arm was caught in the nylon cape. Hélène put the cup down on the curlers tray and glided over to Bunty.

"He said vagina, Kath. On my sofa."

"I blame the lessons, Bunt. We didn't have that chemistry of course. Cookery we had."

"Oh, they go straight into mating now."

"Gravy. First thing I learnt. Stood me in good stead."

The towel Hélène had draped around Jane's shoulders slipped off. Drops from her hair pattered onto her cape. They couldn't sink into the drip-dry material. They stayed on the surface for a while until they glided into the folds.

"And Barb's got that blood pressure."

"Ooh, that can be nasty."

"Well, she shouldn't play so much whist. They don't half get through the pork scratchings."

Jane freed her working hand to lift a magazine. The problem page admonished a mistress. *Married men are sacrosanct. Off-limits*, berated the agony-aunt.

Jane imagined married men in cages like battery hens. When Peter Whitehead rattled his marital bars hard, Jane had set him free for twenty years of preening and strutting in her yard. No need to scratch for corn. She'd fed him from the kernel of her heart. Eager and grateful at first, he'd grown plump and self-satisfied. Cock of the walk.

"June's expecting again, Bunt. Rather her than me, eh? At her age, the Change must be round the corner."

"Don't count your chickens, Kath. Haven't had your tubes tied, have you?"

"Oh stop it, Bunt. My breeding days are over."

Jane could smell the bus fumes fingering under the door and hear last night's vinegary chip litter rasping against it.

Bunty lumbered to the basin. *Do you hold your breath in anticipation, Bunty?* Jane wondered. But Bunty had her Keith. His fingers hiked over her hummocks and into her valleys at night. Monumental mounds to mountaineer, but he knew them like a Sherpa, according to Bunty.

Jane's arm tingled, sharp pecking sensations that faded to nothing. Numbness; as if a wooden limb were tacked to her shoulder. Solid, but dead.

She wanted to call out, but Bunty would fuss and cluck. Kath would light a cigarette and mutter about menopause. Hélène would take charge and everything would shift.

Jane would have to answer questions, lie down, hair wet and feet up, in the back room where Hélène wore rubber gloves to mix tints. It was like a surgeon's room, stiff with gowns and plastic bowls. Jane shivered.

"And his voice is breaking, Kath. It's like having Ian Paisley in the house."

"Is he Irish then? Thought your lot came from Ruislip."

Jane's mouth felt parched. She let the magazine slide and picked up the cup with her working hand. It weighed a hundredweight. Her mouth didn't open. Tea slithered from her lips. She must have drunk a million cups of tea in her life. Why couldn't this be like all the rest? This was *Monday*, for heaven's sake, the day she savoured; the day that refused to hang empty, whining at her like a forgotten swing in the wind.

"Long trousers now, Kath. And fuzz on his top lip."

"Almost a man then."

"Yes, I get him to change plugs for me."

"He'll have picked up those hormones."

"Yes, they're what make his feet stink."

Bunty's voice boomed from the basin. Hélène capped and uncapped bottles. Kath's smoke unfurled in the dust-smitten sun pressing through the blinds.

Peter Whitehead's chest was smooth and white like fresh milk. His wife used that blue speckled powder in her washing machine, so he always smelt of his home. When he used to fall asleep on Thursday afternoons in Jane's bed, she would bury her face in his jersey and wish. She wished throughout the entire twenty years of his achievements that kept precluding them from running to Paradise. Twenty years of his promotions. Babies one, two and three. Extensions one and two. And a thousand hollow promises.

"A good bone is all a wife needs."

"Sorry Kath?"

"A medium carrot and a couple of small onions."

"I'm not with you, love."

"For your basic stock."

"Oh, absolutely, duck."

Jane felt dribble travel down her chin. Her eyes blurred, as if rain was falling through them. She put her good hand to her face and traced her lips. One up, one down. Lopsided. Her face was dying.

Peter Whitehead used to push his fingers into the corners of her mouth to force a smile. He said he would never leave her sad. He didn't realise a smile meant nothing. It was just muscles moving. Like the ones that made you gossip or shiver or thrust out a baby.

Bunty rolled back to her seat. Her bottom oozed into it, juddering the metal legs.

"Soon we'll be new women, Jane. Not that my Keith will ever notice. Mondays only mean corned beef hash and bar billiards at The Spotted…Jane?"

Jane drifted, but saw the changing faces several times. She heard Bunty speak on the telephone. Her voice, rich as fruit loaf, was requesting emergency help. Who was the help for? Where was Hélène?

Kath, hair streaming in two curtains either side of her yellowed face, came close and told her not to worry. Her tobacco-brown

voice betrayed no tremor of doubt. Jane wished she could curl into
Kath's lap and bury her face in the familiar mustard cardigan.

The basin's plughole babbled like hospital machinery beeping
a rhythm.

Jane strayed again, back to the hospital, her baby in her arms.
Nurses plumped pillows and a teacup chinked in its saucer. A
nurse at the end of the bed mopped her with cool wads of watery
cotton wool, slid a pad into place and smoothed the starched gown
beneath her. Another came to massage her stubborn milk away.
Fingers traced her stitches, untwisted her blankets and dimmed
the lights.

Jane longed to stay, but she swam back to the beaky face of an
ambulance man, bluish from blunt razors and fatigue. His mouth
moved slowly. Bunty and Kath stood behind him, holding her
towel and gown between them in a bundle. She felt cold. Naked.
He put a mask over her face. She heard a few words.

Was she married? Next of kin?

She heard Bunty saying no. And Kath saying no one.

So she was a spinster called Jane Frampton?

Yes. That had always been her name.

Jane wished she could tell them there was once a man for
twenty years. A man called Peter Whitehead. Not much of a man.
Pallid and smooth like bottle-fed veal. Lily-livered, Bunty would
call him. And there was a child. A child born with brown hair, like
a damp calf, and hands that Jane held to her face, to her lips. A
child whose breath sighed with sweet milk, whose new skin she
stroked with lanolin lather, dusted with powder and salted with
tears. Jane Frampton's baby.

Where was Hélène? That other childless spinster? Except she
had changed her name a little. Added the 'e' and the accents.
Dropped her surname. Opened the salon. Served tea and
conditioner. Coffee and cream rinse. Tucked her charges in their
gowns and cradled their heads in her basin.

190

No one could take away Hélène's needy family. After Jane and Bunty and Kath on Mondays, there were Carole, June and Janette on Tuesdays. All week she rubbed and patted and made people smile.

Bunty's hair was drying in a frizz. Curlers waited.

Jane had washed her child's birth-bloodied hair. Blotted it dry and watched it become fluff so fine, the hospital light shone through it. She took home the bottle of clear shampoo. It reflected many times in the jointed mirrors of her dressing-table.

"Bunt, do you think she'll have any life at all after this?"

"No idea, Kath. Dear oh dear. Let's give them her handbag and scarf."

Jane surfaced once more before she was moved to the stretcher. She spotted Hélène in the back room, pulling tufts of old hair from brushes.

"Not being funny, Kath, but Jane looks rough without her set."

"Let's hope Hélène will finish ours."

Peter Whitehead hadn't come to hold her when their child was taken away. He had sent a letter telling her about a holiday in Majorca. Holiday abroad number five. They were moving after that, he wrote. It had been good, being with Jane, but he felt a bit trapped. He would think of her often and with affection. Sorry not to visit, but hospitals upset him.

Jane wanted to reach out to the ladies who stood there dripping wet and clutching her things, but her brain was closing. Black and white fragments sifted in her mind, torn scraps that once formed a picture.

The last thing she felt were the tender hands lifting her onto the stretcher, strong fingers applying the oxygen mask, stroking wet hair back from her brow.

She breathed hard, until she was floating and warm. It was not a recovery, she knew.

"Not being funny, but she never said much did she? Bit stuck-up."

"Nothing to say, was there Bunt? No husband and kids. Doesn't leave much."

"Never spoke to Hélène either, did she? Just came for the half-price shampoo and set."

"No nerves in hair, are there Bunt?"

"True, Kath. No more feeling than there is in that basin over there."

The ambulance man took Jane out. Hélène returned.

"I'll shift Carole Whitehead from Tuesdays," she said, reaching for the appointments book. "She's been wanting Mondays for a long time."

Hélène collected her comb and turned up the radio. The basin stopped gurgling.

ACKNOWLEDGEMENTS

Thank you to Adrian, Alexandra, Olivia and Georgia for your steadfast bolstering, unwavering reassurance, brilliant technical support and constant love.

Anthony Howcroft and Sara-Mae Tuson for making this book possible and the entire process of publication so enjoyable.

Jilly Cooper for her kind and supportive words and for giving me so much of her time.

Peter Meinke for his inspiring poetry.

Judy Kidd for always showing such keen interest.

Clare Cooper, Gaynor Davies, Jo Derrick, Jan Fortune-Wood, Rob Richardson, Jill Mannion and Kay Green, for your faith in my stories.

Joe Melia, for his championship of the short story form.

Kath McGurl, who began it all, and fellow bloggers Rosemary, Teresa, Frances, Joanne, Vikki, Lindsay, Suzanne, Sallie, Wendy and Tracy for their endless encouragement.

Julia Anderson, Katie Carr and Bernadette James for their belief in my writing.

Kevin and Claire in Bisley village shop for their enthusiasm.

My parents, John and Betty Hill, for all the Saturday half-crowns spent in WH Smith.

And Mrs Goldwater, my nursery school teacher from many moons ago, for letting me stay inside at playtime to teach myself to read.

'When Planets Slip Their Tracks'
First published in *The Coastal Zoo*, 2014

'Cherry's Stain'
First published in *Significant Spaces*, 2012

'Before Last Wednesday'
First published in *The Yellow Room*, 2012

'Decisions Made Over Madeleine's Toast'
Prizewinning story in *Southport Writers' Circle competition*, 2012

'Wind and Water'
First published in *The Bristol Short Story Prize Anthology*, 2013

'Big Day Out'
First published in *On The Bench*, 2014

'The Reliable Sitter'
First published in *Five Stop Story*, 2012

'The Invitation'
First published in *Ways Of Falling*, 2010

'One-Horse Town'
First published in *Writers' Forum*, 2008

'Quiston Avenue'
First published in *From Barcelona to Bihar*, 2012

'The Biology Lesson'
Prizewinning story in the *Scottish Association of Writers* competition, 2013

'Aurora and the Book Trolley'
First published in *Reaching Out*, 2013

'The Revival Of Clara Petacci'
Prizewinning story in the *William Trevor/Elizabeth Bowen Short Story Competition*, 2013

'Michael's List Of Fears'
Prizewinning story in the *Grace Dieu Writers' Circle Competition*, 2011

'The English Lesson'
First published in *The Lampeter Review*, 2014

'The Long Drive'
Short-listed in the *William Trevor/Elizabeth Bowen Short Story Competition*, 2012

'Bonanza Tully's Baby'
First published in *A Roof Of Red Tiles*, 2011

'Following Candace'
First published in *The Salt Anthology of New Writing*, 2013

'Opening Time'
First published by *Ink Tears*, 2012

'Ten O'clock to Balham'
First published in *Jericho*, 2012

'Before The Birds Sing'
First published in *Flair News* magazine, 2011

'Half-Price Mondays With Hélène'
First published in *The Yellow Room*, 2011

NOBODY WILL EVER LOVE YOU
by Anthony Howcroft

Short stories are like miniature films, and this prizewinning collection by A M Howcroft delivers a potent screening of arthouse tales and Hollywood blockbusters. They are studded with a memorable cast of characters, such as a chicken-factory worker balanced high on a slippery roof, a woman carving saints out of driftwood, teenage boy-racers who've solved life's mysteries, through to a business woman who dies nine times. Each story is set within a rich-cinematic backdrop to reveal people at critical turning points, with delicately balanced risks and rewards. Whether starting riots in Paris, breaking into a friend's house in California, or killing time before being busted by customs officers, the narrators are flawed, unpredictable, smart and stupid in equal measure. Funny, moving and often provoking, these compelling stories will entertain; giving you images that linger and dialogue you'll want to repeat in fake accents.

An exciting new talent who really knows how to write and keep the reader thoroughly engaged.

Katie Fforde

BOYFRIENDS
by Bonnie West

In her debut collection, Bonnie West transforms everyday experiences into events that are complex, sometimes heart wrenching, and frequently unexpected. The collection includes stories of teenagers with an unabashed naiveté and contagious belief that they are indeed invincible; and stories of adults who are not so unlike their teenage counterparts as they follow their hearts into compromising positions. As perceptive and observant as West's characters are, they often over-estimate their knowledge, sharing a degree of honesty even when they delude themselves. A woman falling in love with a chicken, an angry pathologist, or a ghost at the edge of the woods seem unlikely scenarios, but as we read these stories we come to believe anything is possible. Throughout the collection, West's observations are piercing, irreverent, and often very funny.

Brilliant stories that zing with humor and then break your heart – until you laugh out loud again.

Robin Black, author *If I Loved You I Would Tell You This*

InkTears

"I love to read but I'm too busy."
"The last time I read a story I was on holiday."

If this sounds familiar then you might be like us. We love to read fiction but the modern world makes it hard to find the time. We can help.

At InkTears we want people to rediscover the pleasure of reading in a way that fits their lifestyle. We send a short story every month to our readers via email, free of charge. The story takes less than ten minutes to read. If you want you can give the writer direct feedback on their story, and join in our active community. Or you can just enjoy reading something other than email – it's entirely your choice.

Extend your horizons. Join today to start receiving your tales, and see what the short story can offer.

Short fiction for busy people
www.inktears.com